The Ros...o...ita...ce

MARY TANT

The Rossington Inheritance

Threshold Press

First published 2007
First paperback edition 2008
published by
Threshold Press Ltd, Norfolk House
75 Bartholomew Street, Newbury
Berks RG14 5DU
Phone 01635-230272 and fax 01635-44804
email: publish@threshold-press.co.uk
www.threshold-press.co.uk

ISBN 978-1-903152-21-8

Printed in England by Biddles Ltd, Kings Lynn

FOR MY PARENTS
WHO ENCOURAGED ME
IN ALL MY INTERESTS

Rossington manor and priory

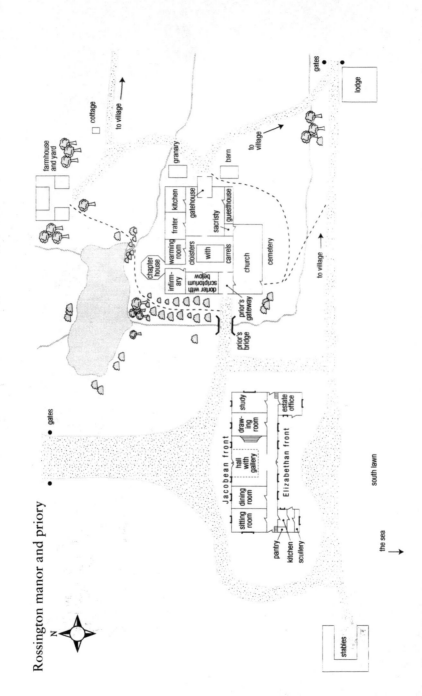

Roscombe village

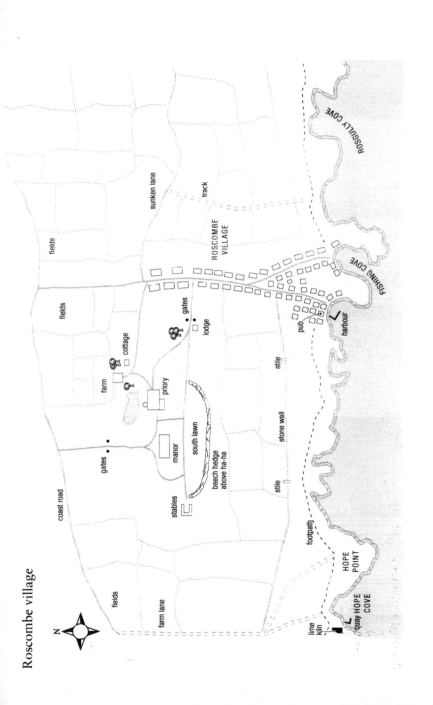

ONE

Lucy wiped the paintbrush carefully on an old rag and laid it down. She put the lid firmly back onto the paint tin, pressing it down with her foot to make sure it was closed. Then she straightened up, pushing her heavy chestnut hair back from her face with one paint-smeared hand, adding more white streaks to those that already marked her small lightly-tanned features. 'That's it, Will,' she called, 'they're all done.'

The slight wiry boy crouched on the gravel drive looked across at her and grinned. He stood up and threw his handful of weeds into the heavy galvanised bucket beside him, which was already brimming over with tufts of grass and clumps of plantain. He sauntered across the lawn to where she stood, a smile splitting his thin face as he saw how bespattered with paint she was.

'You won't have any difficulty going on the war path,' he observed.

Lucy shrugged impatiently. 'You can't make omelettes without breaking eggs,' she countered tartly, and gestured about her. 'What do you think?'

Will turned slowly round, viewing the south lawn. It was dotted with deceptively casual groups of cast-iron chairs and tables, newly painted in white. A few cedar benches, shining with freshly-applied linseed oil, were backed carefully against the beech hedge which separated the lawn from the ha-ha.

'They do look good, Lucy. What a shame we can't eat them!' He glanced at her out of the corner of his eye, and then went on hurriedly, 'But what about the rest of it?' He pointed at the molehills that showed in places through the long grass of the lawn, and at the branches arching luxuriantly from the overgrown hedge.

'Oh, that'll be alright. Bert's going to see to it all when he's finished edging the drive.'

'This year?' muttered Will, avoiding his sister's gaze as she eyed him suspiciously, not quite sure of what he had said.

'Well, anyway, the house looks fine, doesn't it?' she asked him, looking proudly across the drive to the south front of the old house. Indeed, it did look particularly attractive, with the spring sunlight warming the mellow red bricks and sparkling on the leaded windows.

'Let's hope they don't see that the windows are loose and the roof leaks,' Will said gloomily.

'Must you be so pessimistic?' Lucy snapped crossly.

Her brother was immediately repentant. 'I'm sorry. It's just that I know so well what's wrong with it. But it does really look good, and, honestly, no one else will see all the bad things, not even if they need to have their teas in the hall.'

'No, they're not likely to,' Lucy agreed, her irritation forgotten. 'It's lucky we can use it if the weather is bad.'

Will opened his mouth, and then quickly closed it again, deciding that further comment would be unwise. Lucy had not noticed, and began to run over her arrangements again.

'I've got in six different kinds of tea, so there's plenty of choice. It'll be interesting to see what people like best. They're all leaf tea, but I've got some herb and fruit tea-bags too.' She caught Will's eye as he made a face. 'You must remember how keen Heinrich was on peppermint tea after meals when he stayed here with Daddy.'

Will nodded, but did not feel he should comment. Lucy

waited a second and then went on, 'You know that Tilly ran a teashop for a time. Well, she said that it wouldn't be economical to provide milk in jugs and butter in dishes, because you could never know how many people would come and when. She always used packets.'

Will snorted, and Lucy nodded. 'That's what I thought, so we'll try it properly at first and see how it goes.'

She paused to consider for a minute. 'Gran is busy in the kitchen. She's promised to have the freezer full of cakes and biscuits, so that it will just be scones to make freshly. No,' she added, poking her brother in the ribs, 'she's not making them for you to eat, pig.'

'Oh, go on, Lucy, weeding that drive is killing me. I'm just about starving.'

'Well, maybe when you've finished,' she said hardheartedly, 'Gran will find you something.'

Will groaned. 'But it's going to take ages. I might just as well have stayed at Gudwal's and risked getting the lurgy. I'd probably get more to eat in the sick bay, and I wouldn't have to work so hard either.'

Lucy ignored him. 'Simon's bringing up the crockery this morning.' She glanced at her watch. 'Soon, I expect. He's being very good about it, you know. He's not charging us for the things he's made, because if we display one of his cards he's likely to get a lot more customers.' Will snorted again and Lucy turned on him angrily. 'It *is* good of him,' she reiterated. 'It would cost us quite a lot to pay for four dozen sets of cups, saucers and plates, let alone all the rest of the stuff.'

'He's probably trying to get round you,' Will muttered cynically.

Lucy flushed. 'Why should he?' she demanded.

'Well, for a start, I bet he wants to get you on his side about this detecting business. Graham was really mad when he found him down by the lake.'

'I can't see that it matters,' Lucy retorted defiantly. 'If he does mention it, I shall tell him he can take his metal detector wherever he likes in the grounds.'

'Well, Graham won't be pleased, that's all I can say, and for once I think he's right.' Will sounded annoyed, and as a thought struck him he added darkly, 'I bet he thinks Simon's going to find the old monks' treasure.'

'It would be a good thing if he did,' Lucy declared. 'We wouldn't have to worry about all this then.' She waved her arm generally in the direction of the house.

'Huh, the only things he's ever found have been real rubbish. I wasted a whole morning going over the south field with him, and all we found were rusty old bits of metal that he said were nails from horseshoes, and bits of broken plough. Not even an old coin.'

'There you are then,' Lucy said triumphantly. 'It can't do any harm to let him look around.'

An outburst of loud barking made them both turn quickly. The door in the west kitchen wing was only slightly open, but a large black curly-haired mongrel squeezed through it and erupted into the courtyard. He rushed past them to stand barking defiantly at the green Morris van that was picking its way slowly up the gravel drive. A small brown and white spaniel came racing after the bigger dog, and stood beside him adding her shrill yapping to the general hubbub.

'I'm off,' Will said abruptly, after a quick look at the van. 'Hugh's bird-watching up on the cliffs, and he said he'd show me how to use that long-distance lens on his camera.' He turned away before his sister could say anything, and added over his shoulder, 'You'd better hang on to Juno, she can be a pest if we're busy.'

Whistling up Hades, so that the black dog came bounding eagerly after him, he strode across the lawn, skirted the beech hedge and jumped over the ha-ha, leaving Lucy to scoop up the indignant Juno and wait for the van to stop.

I wonder where he is, Will thought, slowing down once he

was out of earshot of the house. He brightened up as he remembered that Hugh had mentioned the cormorants, and his step quickened as he crossed the fields towards the cliff path. The cormorants were likely to be digesting their catch and drying their wings, perched on the ridges of the Devil's Teeth like a group of prehistoric creatures.

The cliff path was separated from the fields by a low stone wall, which was patched with a natural quilt of multifarious lichens. The primroses nestling in the shelter of the wall were already opening their pale flowers in the warm sunshine, and Will noticed them as he climbed the wall, using the stones which jutted out as steps. Lucy would be pleased, he thought, she wanted flowers to put on the tables.

Although he had scrambled up the steps as a puppy, Hades disdained them now and sprang effortlessly over the wall to join his master on the cliff path. Will turned to the west and Hades bounded eagerly ahead of him, disturbing some dozy early bees which circled just above him.

The dog snuffled happily over the short turf and through the clumps of heather, his long tail waving wildly as he poked his nose into innumerable holes. Seagulls drifted in circles on the air currents above them, white against the clear blue sky. Below them the sea gleamed in facets of turquoise, emerald and sapphire, while the breakers pounded unseen rocks beneath the cliff, so that there was a constant booming roar in Will's ears and spray was flung high in a fine mist.

The cliff path rose steeply ahead of them as they approached Hope Point. Will scrambled up the zig-zag route with the ease born of long practice, passing Hades who had stopped to drink noisily at the stream that burbled down from the heights. Hades, though, did not like following in second place, and he shadowed Will closely, breathing hotly on his heels, waiting for a chance to overtake and gain the lead once more. Will soon grew tired of this and trod off the rocky path onto the springy scented thyme, allowing Hades to bound joyfully past.

They reached the more level ground at the back of the Point, and Will turned, as he always did, to look down on the valley where his home lay. The red Tudor manor house had been built by Harry Rossington when he acquired the priory and its lands from Henry VIII, and now lay glowing warmly against the surrounding greenery. West and east wings sheltered the stone-flagged courtyard, where two small figures moved backwards and forwards from the green van to the large oak door in the centre of the house. When a third figure came out of the estate office in the east wing and stopped to speak to them, Will grimaced and looked beyond them.

From this angle he could not see the grandiose white Jacobean front and porch that one of his many times great-grandfathers had imposed on the north front of the house. The family had often felt grateful that he died before he had time to implement the other fashionable changes he had planned for the interior. None of his successors had shown a similar urge to alter their home, or perhaps they all had more pressing demands on their income.

North east of the house, a hint of spring green brightened the scattered clumps of oak trees protecting the home farm beyond the lake, which shone like polished steel. A narrow tree-lined brook flowed south from the lake, and circled east below the crenellated tower of the little church, which still doughtily guarded the old Cistercian priory buildings. As Will's gaze followed the line of the brook eastward alongside the back drive a flight of rooks flew raggedly in over the uneven slate roofs of the village and alighted beside the nests in the tall beeches opposite the lodge. The ensuing cawing and flurry were faintly audible where he stood.

A louder, nearer, sound of frenzied barking disturbed Will's reverie, and he spun round to see Hades at the far end of the Point. He was bouncing up and down with glee, darting ecstatically forward to lick the face of a man sitting comfortably against a large boulder. Fending off the excited dog with a tolerant arm, the man looked around and, catching sight of Will, waved to him. 'Come and keep this wild animal of yours quiet, will you?' he asked Will, as the boy approached.

Will grabbed Hades' collar and pushed him down onto the short-cropped turf, where he lay, sides heaving, pink tongue lolling out of the corner of his mouth. 'Stay!' Will said sternly, and Hades looked up at him for a second, bright eyes gleaming, before Will took his hand away. 'He'll be alright now,' the boy said. 'I'm sorry if he disturbed the birds.'

'No problem,' Hugh replied. He pointed towards the sharp rim of rocks which trailed out from the cliff into the sea. Cormorants stood on the ledges of the rocks, shuffling their feet, furling and unfurling their wings, as they stared up towards the Point. 'They'll settle down again pretty quickly if he stays quiet, but anyway I've already got some good shots of them fishing and drying their wings. They've been flying in for the last hour or so.' He glanced down at Will enquiringly. 'I wasn't expecting you today; I thought you had a lot of work to do at home.'

Will shrugged. 'I have. Lucy wants the drive weeded and raked before she starts doing teas at Easter. It's a hell of a job, and I needed a break. Besides, that potter bloke has just come up to the house and there's going to be one almighty row about his metal detecting.'

'Oh?' Hugh raised an eyebrow.

'Yeah, you bet. Graham was absolutely wild when he found him working round by the lake, said he hadn't got permission and was trespassing. We've hardly heard about anything else since, but Lucy's still going to let him use his detector in the grounds. I hope she's not soft on him,' he added gloomily.

Hugh grinned. 'You don't like him, do you?'

'No, I don't,' Will was very definite. 'And neither does Hades. But if she marries him he'll probably come and live with us. Coming home for the holidays just won't be the same, if he's going to be around all the time. I don't expect I'll ever be able to get rid of him.'

'Well, even if your sister does marry him, I don't expect she'll want to live with you indefinitely,' Hugh pointed out with a smile.

'Oh, she's alright, I don't really mind if she does. She's pretty decent, actually,' he confided. 'She got a first-class degree in botany, you know, and she was offered a grant to survey rainforest plants in Peru for two years. She didn't take it up, though, because Dad died, and the house and estate are in a pretty bad way. No money,' he said succinctly. 'So she came home with these schemes to make some. Teas first and then later paying guests – after we've fixed the roof.'

'Can't you sell the place?' Hugh asked curiously.

The boy was silent for a minute, gazing out over the sea. 'Well, it's entailed, but I suppose we could find a way if we really wanted to, but we haven't seriously considered it. You see, it's always been home to us, and we're rather fond of it. Dad was away a lot and I don't remember my mother, although Lucy can, a little. She died just after I was born. I heard Gran say once that she thought that was why Dad travelled so much.'

Will watched a narrow black shape flying straight as an arrow to the rocks, where its arrival caused a rippling eddy among the resting birds, as they shifted to make space for the newcomer. 'Anyway,' he said, 'it wasn't so bad about the money when he was alive because he earned quite a lot from his books. But now, what with paying death duties as well, it's a bit sticky. Still, Graham reckons the income from the estate will keep us ticking over until I'm twenty-one, and that'll be in just over five years.'

The boy looked at Hugh seriously and continued, 'Graham's always looked after the estate, he grew up with my father, you know, and Gran says that he probably cares more about the place than Dad did. I'm not sure, though.' He was silent again for a while, before concluding, 'Anyway, we wouldn't want to sell it.'

Hades stirred at their feet, whimpering in excitement. They

both turned to see a slender figure emerging from the cliff path onto the headland. 'It's Lucy,' Will exclaimed, getting to his feet and calling her name. Hades bounded over to her and she looked round, startled. Will ran over to where she stood, thick chestnut hair blown by the wind from the sea, cheeks deeply flushed with more than the exertion of the climb, and eyes bright with anger. She stroked Hades absent-mindedly as he snuffled round her feet. 'What is it, Lucy? What's happened?' Will demanded anxiously.

'Oh, it's nothing, just Graham going off the deep end,' she said shortly, pushing Hades away as he tried to jump up.

'About Simon and the metal detecting?' Will queried, already sure of the answer.

'Of course. He's completely besotted with the idea that there's something valuable to find. I sometimes wonder if he really believes that old story of the monks' treasure. But he's got no right to imply that Simon would be dishonest about his finds.'

She paused and noticed the man standing behind Will for the first time. Of medium height and build, with brown hair and eyes, wearing old brown trousers and a cream-coloured pullover, he seemed to her to have appeared from nowhere. She stared at him in surprise and caught her breath.

Will followed the direction of her eyes. 'Oh, Lucy, this is Hugh. Hugh, this is my sister Lucy.'

Lucy recovered her composure and held out her hand. 'Hi. I've heard a great deal about you from Will.'

Hugh smiled faintly as he shook her hand. 'Hello. I can say the same; Will is full of your plans. I shall certainly have to come to tea when you open the venture. At Easter, isn't it?'

She smiled ruefully. 'I hope so, but it's only a few weeks away now. I sometimes wonder if we'll ever be ready in time, and whether anyone will come anyway.'

'If the basic elements are there, you'll be alright. It won't matter if the inessential things aren't all done when you start.'

Will brightened as he heard this, convinced that weeding the drive was not likely to be essential, and listened to the conversation with more attention.

'People will come to try it as something new,' Hugh said, 'or because they've heard of Mrs Rossington's baking, which is famous locally, you know. Once they've been they'll keep coming back, because the quality of the food is going to be a big attraction. On top of that, you've got a fantastic setting.' He gestured down into the valley. 'The monks always chose their sites well.'

Lucy glanced at him curiously. 'Do you know a lot about old monasteries?' she asked.

He met her eyes for a moment. 'A little, no more than most,' he said.

'You do, too,' Will exclaimed indignantly. 'Lots more than most people. You should come and talk to Graham. He always likes telling people about the old priory.'

'But not today,' Lucy said quickly. She hesitated, but then carried on, 'I've rather upset him today by giving someone from the village permission to use a metal detector in the grounds.' She looked up at Hugh. 'I expect you know him. Simon is the potter who lives at the Old Wheelwright's cottage.'

'I've come across him,' Hugh replied. 'Do you know him well?'

'He's been here a couple of years, but I've really only got to know him recently, since I've been home. He's a very good potter.' She turned to Will, who was tussling with Hades. 'The crockery he brought up is a lovely creamy yellow, it will look good on the tables. Tilly wanted him to let her paint flowers on it, but I'm glad he didn't; it's just right as it is.' She turned back to Hugh. 'More visitors will be good for him too, because his pottery is a bit isolated in the village – the road doesn't go anywhere.'

'That's the beauty of it,' said Hugh. 'You're in an ideal spot here, in a sheltered valley near the sea. If the road led somewhere the village would have been developed long ago. Another plus for the monks; they always preferred isolated sites, as long as there was running water, and you've got plenty of that.'

Lucy smiled. 'You really do know a bit about them.' She paused for a moment. 'Look, would you like to come to tea today and meet Graham. He'd love to tell you about the priory.' She made a rueful face. 'He really knows much more about it than we do, and he doesn't often get a truly interested audience.'

Hugh raised one of his eyebrows. 'I'm to be the peace offering?' he asked softly.

Lucy flushed and then, catching his eye, smiled again. 'Well, yes, if you like. But,' she added quickly, slightly flustered, 'we'd like you to come too. Today or any day,' she hurried on, then stopped abruptly.

Will came unwittingly to her rescue. 'Yes, we would,' he said, pushing Hades off and scrambling to his feet. 'Do come today, you can sample Gran's cakes.' His sister's face lit up with amusement and he glared at her. 'And I'll show you where the barn owl nests; it's in the granary by the priory gatehouse.' He grinned. 'You'll be seeing that anyway, although you must have passed it already; I expect Graham will show you round the place, unless you get out of it.'

'How can I refuse so many attractions? Yes, I'd love to come this afternoon.' Hugh said, looking at Lucy. 'As long as it's not to be a burnt offering.' He paused, but she refused to rise to the bait. 'Are you going on, or would you like to stay and have some coffee with us?' He gestured to where his rucksack lay on the grass near the boulder.

She hesitated. 'I'd love to, but I should get back,' she replied reluctantly. 'I've got to finish the wording for the roadside signs.' She turned back down the path, waving goodbye before disappearing from their view.

Will began to return with Hugh to the sun-warmed rocks on the promontory, but he suddenly stopped. 'I ought to go back too,' he said abruptly. 'There's a lot to do, and as I've got away from school a couple of weeks early it's not fair to leave it all to Lucy.' He looked up at Hugh. 'You don't mind, do you?'

'No, of course I don't, Will,' Hugh said. 'I can show you how to use the long-distance lens another day. You go off now, and I'll see you this afternoon.'

Will flashed a quick smile at him and ran quickly over the headland and down the cliff path after his sister. He was followed shortly by an indignant Hades who had been busy tracing a scent and had not seen his master leave.

Lucy opened the manor's front door to Hugh when he rang the large ship's bell that hung outside. As he stepped from the outdoor brightness into the comparative gloom of the panelled hall, he noticed appreciatively that she had changed out of her paint-spattered jeans and smock into a leaf-green jersey skirt and a cream shirt, with a green patterned scarf tucked into its collar.

She gestured around the hall. 'This was the basis of the original prior's house, with a room on either side. The oak panelling is Elizabethan, and was put in when the house was extended by Harry Rossington, after he'd bought the property from the king. He put in the gallery too,' she said, pointing above their heads. 'This is what's mentioned in most of the architectural guides; it's what the enthusiasts like to see. When he was little, Will used to sit up there and giggle over what they said down here.'

Lucy smiled suddenly, an unexpectedly mischievous gamine smile. 'And that's my contribution to the guided tour of the premises. Come down to the sitting room. Will is just coming, he's washing after a massive attack on the weeds in the drive, and Gran is bringing in a selection of cakes which will restore his energy immediately.'

She led him down the corridor on the west, pausing to show him the dining room. 'This was one of the original rooms in the prior's house. The one on the other side of the hall we use as a drawing room.'

Hugh looked round the half-panelled room, admiring the cream-coloured walls which accentuated the massive stone fire-place in the east wall, and the soft green curtains hanging at the mullioned windows, which drew colours from the worn rugs on the polished oak floors. A few portraits hung on the walls, and miscellaneous pictures – two sea-battles, one hunting scene and an enormous prize ram.

'It's just right,' he said quietly to the girl beside him. 'Who chose the colours?'

'My mother,' she replied softly. 'Daddy wouldn't ever change anything, so the colours were always repeated when we decorated.'

She turned away and he followed her to the sitting room next door, enjoying the comfortable welcome the room offered as he entered. Muted yellow walls and gentian blue curtains framed a comfortable jumble of armchairs and tapestry-seated upright chairs clustered around the fireplace. Sunlight poured through the west-facing French windows, highlighting colours in the room. The central table was large and low, and relatively clear, but the other tables in the room, in a variety of heights and sizes, were thickly covered with magazines, books and newspapers.

He was aware suddenly that Lucy was waiting, watching him as he absorbed the room's appearance and he looked across at her, meeting her eyes. He was about to speak when a telephone bell rang shrilly. 'I'm sorry, I'd better go and answer that,' she said. 'Make yourself comfortable.'

He stood aside to let her pass through the doorway, and stayed where he was, listening to her footsteps retreating down the corridor back to the hall. He moved slowly into the room, savouring the atmosphere, drawn to the cluttered bookshelves, where he began to look over the titles of the books. His eye-brows rose, and he took out a worn leather-bound book and looked at the title page, before turning the pages carefully, stopping here and there to read a section with some pleasure. He became engrossed and only came to himself with a start a little while later when he heard a slight noise in the room.

He turned round, one finger automatically keeping his place in the book, to find that Mrs Rossington had come into the room. On the tea table was the tray she had brought in, heavily laden with lemon and ginger biscuits and a large Victoria sponge with cream and jam enticingly sandwiched between the layers. She was a slender woman in her mid-sixties, with iron-grey hair cut severely short in a bob which framed her sallow pointed face. Her bright eyes were surveying him curiously, and she smiled as she held her hand out to him. 'Hello,' she said. 'I'm Isobel Rossington.'

He smiled back at her and his tanned face suddenly acquired a striking charm. As he looked at her it was easy for him to see the resemblance that her grandchildren bore to her. They both had her build, but while Lucy spoke in the same quiet definite tones, he suspected that Will had inherited more of her outgoing manner. He stepped forward and took her outstretched hand. 'How do you do. I'm Hugh Carey.' His smile widened. 'After meeting your grandchildren I believe I would have recognised you anywhere.'

Her dark eyes shone with amusement, and for an instant she recaptured something of the beauty that had been hers. 'Yes, they have both inherited characteristics from the Penleighs, my family, but they both have the Rossington determination too, which is just as well. Their father was all Rossington,' she added, and then glanced at the book he still held.

'Aubrey's *Brief Lives*,' he said, holding the book up for her to see. 'One of my favourites.'

She nodded. 'My husband's too. He collected most of these.' She smiled a little. 'The Rossingtons are an active breed and in his final years he suffered rather a lot as a result of war wounds. Fortunately he was able to turn his energies to searching out the books he enjoyed.'

Hugh said hesitantly. 'Mrs Rossington, it's no concern of mine, but this is a rare book and there are many others here, some of them first editions.' He paused and she smiled at him encouragingly, so he continued, 'They are likely to be worth a great deal of money.'

'You're wondering why we don't sell them?' she asked in her usual forthright manner. 'Well, as a last resort perhaps we shall have to, but Lucy is quite insistent that all of Will's inheritance must be kept intact, and the Rossingtons are very determined.'

She caught the conflicting emotions that briefly showed in his face, and added, 'Not to say stubborn.' She turned as Hades bounded into the room, barking happily. 'Hades! No!'

Hugh caught the big dog's paws as he jumped up in greeting, and pushed him back down. 'No, Hades, down!' The dog's tail lashed backwards and forwards wildly, and he thrust his nose into Hugh's hand, as Will came through the doorway.

'Will,' his grandmother said, 'come and make Hades behave or he'll have to go out. Where's Juno? Ah, there she is,' she added as the little spaniel followed the boy into the room and hesitated nervously at sight of the stranger. Reassured by Hades' enthusiasm she advanced and sniffed cautiously at Hugh's shoes. Convinced at last of his integrity, her feathery tail began to wave furiously too, and she licked his hand as he bent down to stroke her.

'I'm sorry, Gran,' Will said apologetically. 'He heard Hugh and came racing in.' He took Hades by the collar and pushed him towards the rug in front of the fireplace. 'Go on, Hades, lie down.' Reluctantly the black dog allowed himself to be taken away from Hugh, and flung himself heavily down on the rug, where he was soon joined by the dainty Juno.

'Where's Lucy?' Will asked, glancing at the tea tray. 'I thought she was here.'

'She was,' Hugh replied, 'but the telephone rang just as we came in, and she went to answer it.'

'Really,' said Isobel, 'I do wish people wouldn't ring at meal times. Still, at least it's not dinner. You'd be surprised how many times Lucy has to leave her food to answer the wretched telephone. Sometimes I'm sorry it was ever invented.' She turned to Will. 'Did you catch who it was when you came through the hall?'

He shook his head. 'I didn't come that way, I came down the west stairs. Do you want me to go and see if I can find out?'

'Yes, that might …' she broke off as her granddaughter came back into the room. 'Who was it this time, dear?'

'Anna,' Lucy replied, brushing a lock of hair away from her face. 'She's at Moreton and wants to come over.' She crossed the room and pulled the French window almost closed. 'It's getting a little chilly, isn't it?'

Isobel was undeterred. 'It wouldn't do that young lady any harm to stay with her father when she does manage to come down.' She sounded surprisingly severe. 'When did she arrive?'

'Yesterday afternoon, I think,' Lucy replied, 'but you know how it is with Anna, she gets bored when she doesn't have plenty to do.'

'Still …' Isobel was interrupted by Will, who exclaimed loudly, 'Oh blow! Is she coming now?'

'Who?' asked a deep voice from the doorway. A rather bulky man of middle height stood there, his thick mane of salt and pepper hair swept back tidily from a solid forehead. He looked round the room slowly and Will greeted him, 'Hello, Graham. Come and meet Hugh. He's potty about old buildings and monks and things, too.'

'We've already met,' said Graham, coming into the room, nodding at Hugh with a smile. Catching sight of Lucy's expression of surprise, he added, with a twinkle in his eyes, 'He does rent an estate cottage, you know.' Turning back to Hugh he asked, 'How are you getting on there?'

'Very well, thank you. It's a snug little place, and quite a secluded spot. It's most convenient to be just outside the village, and close enough to the farm to get fresh milk and eggs.'

Isobel had seated herself at the tea table, and gestured to the rest of the company to sit down. She glanced across at Hugh. 'I'm so glad you go to the farm. Molly Leygar is such a pleasant woman, and she always works so hard too. Life still isn't easy for a farmer's wife.'

'Yes indeed, she always seems to be busy with something whenever I see her, but I don't have to go there very often, only if I want to change my order. As I have a regular order,' he explained as Isobel seemed interested, 'Philly very kindly brings it over for me every day.'

'Ah, I see,' Isobel commented, and meeting the wicked gleam in her dark eyes Hugh was well aware that she did see only too well.

Lucy had followed the conversation, and said quietly, 'I expect she delivers your order at the same time as she brings ours up. She's a nice girl, and likes to get out and about when she can.'

Isobel had poured cups of Indian tea for them all and said, as she passed one to Hugh, 'We always have this for the family, I'm so used to it after my days in India, but we're having to get in some different blends for Lucy's teas.'

Putting his cup down on a gate-leg table by the French windows, Graham seated himself in one of the large wing chairs, accepted a piece of sponge cake, and harked back to the conversation he had caught earlier. 'Who is coming, Will?' he asked.

'Oh, Anna,' Will replied grumpily, casting a proprietorial eye over the tea table. 'You'd never think she'd eat such a lot, but,' he added grudgingly, 'there's plenty here, I suppose.'

Lucy laughed. 'She doesn't eat any more than you do.'

'I know,' Will explained, 'it's just that you'd think she'd be the sort to be always dieting and worrying about getting fat.'

Hugh grinned, but his attention was claimed by Graham, who obviously had no interest in the prospective visitor. 'Do I understand from Will's comment that you are interested in monastic buildings?'

'Well, yes, but only generally; I don't know a great deal about them,' Hugh responded cautiously, ignoring a muffled grunt from Will, whose mouth was full of lemon biscuit.

'You must come and look round the remains of the old priory after tea. You'll find them very interesting, there's a surprising amount left when you know what you're looking at.' Graham leaned forward, shutting Hugh off slightly from the rest of the company.

'It was quite a large priory of the Cistercian house at Ravenstow, with several granges in outlying areas, but it was one of the many that fell into disrepute long before the Dissolution. My Latin is pretty poor, but as far as I can make out from the old records the priory's wealth was originally founded on its sheep runs.'

Graham paused to take a bite of his cake, but quickly resumed his narrative. 'Over the years, though, it developed quite a reputation for its learning. In fact we know the monks made illuminated missals and general religious books for most of the magnates in this area, and sometimes quite a long way further afield too, as late as the end of the fifteenth century. The British Museum has pages from a Book of Hours commissioned by one of the Norfolk Howards, which have been identified with the work of one of the masters from the priory's workshop.' He was now well into his stride, lecturing about his favourite topic, and Hugh, glancing at the other man, was quite sure he knew a great deal about it.

'Still,' Graham continued a little ponderously, and totally oblivious to Hugh's assessment, 'the main wealth of the priory did come from its lands, though, of course, there was very little of them left by the sixteenth century. It's probable that the books and church vessels had all been sold off by then too; it's certain at least that Henry VIII's Commissioners found nothing of value here, even the lead was missing from large parts of the nave roof when they wrote their report after the first visitation.'

'You mention the records,' Hugh said, as the other

man paused for breath. 'How well is the priory's history documented?'

Graham was now completely absorbed in his subject, quite unaware of the other conversations going on around him, and had just absently accepted another slice of cake. He opened his mouth to answer Hugh's question when he was startled by a loud cry from the doorway.

'Darlings, how lovely to see you all! It's been such an age! And tea too, how nice.'

Standing framed in the doorway, lit by the dim light filtering through the leaded panes in the corridor windows, was a young woman. From her curling black hair and rose-tinted cheeks to her dainty feet encased in expensive walking shoes, she was, and knew she was, quite lovely. She flew across the room in a cloud of scented air and kissed Isobel and Lucy affectionately.

'You haven't changed one bit, my pets. That's one of the nice things about coming home, knowing that you and the manor will be just the same. I didn't ring the bell, because I knew where you'd be so I came straight in and here you are.'

She turned to Will, but he had risen to his feet with the others and hastily held out his hand. 'Hello, Anna,' he said repressively.

'Why, Will,' she said admiringly, taking his hand and pressing her delicately-powdered cheek against his reluctant one, 'how you've grown. You must be the only one who has changed.'

He scowled, but Anna had turned away to smile brightly at Graham and murmur a few words to him, which brought a twitch to his firmly-set lips. Then she looked at the man beside him, and her beautiful blue eyes widened in surprise. 'Why, Hugh! Of all the places I never expected to see you! What on earth are you doing here?'

'Hello, Anna,' Hugh replied, taking her proffered hands and kissing her cheek. 'I'm staying in the area for a bit. But what about you? I shouldn't have thought the country was quite your scene.'

She gurgled deliciously with laughter. 'You're quite right, it's not – especially as I'm virtually isolated here. I expect you've already found there's no mobile reception anywhere in the valley.' She sighed theatrically. 'But Daddy lives here so I pop down to see the old boy from time to time. Duty calls, you know, and all that. Besides,' she looked at him ruefully, with her famous smile, 'I'm between roles.'

She accepted a cup of tea from Isobel and, as she saw the expression on that lady's face, said with immediate understanding, 'Yes, Gran Ross, but Daddy wouldn't really like it, you know, if I were to dance attendance on him all the time. He thinks he would, of course, but he'd get terribly irritable, poor darling, if I were there too much.'

The slight frown disappeared from Isobel's forehead, and she smiled. 'I expect you're right, Anna, your father's style of life has always been very placid and I know he doesn't like it upset. But I think he has been a little lonely of late.'

Anna nodded. 'Yes, he was very pleased to see me, but you know he'll soon miss his peace and quiet again. Mmm, yes, please, I'd like a slice of that.' She smiled happily. 'I knew it would be best to come to see you at tea time.' She sank gracefully into an armchair and accepted the plate that Hugh handed her before he sat down nearby, ignoring Will's stunned disapprobation.

Anna glanced across at Lucy. 'This is amazing, you know. Hugh and I were always meeting in London.' Turning back to him she said lightly, 'I shall rely on you for amusement even more here, darling.'

Before she could go on there was a tap on the French window and they all looked up, startled, to see a tall man hovering irresolutely on the threshold. A light breeze was ruffling the fair hair that reached almost to his shoulders, and his eyes looked round the room uncertainly as Hades rushed forward growling.

Anna sprang to her feet with a cry of surprise, and ran

forward too, pushing the French window open and holding out her hands. 'Simon darling, how quickly you've got here.' She drew him into the room past the glowering Hades and turned to Lucy. 'I knew you wouldn't mind if Simon met me here; it's so hard making arrangements when I can't use my mobile. I was looking round his studio this morning and he was telling me all about his metal detecting, so I persuaded him to let me go with him. It sounds very exciting.'

'But of course Simon knows he's always welcome,' Lucy said mendaciously, smiling at him as she studiously ignored Will's deepening scowl and Graham's stiffening figure in the big wing chair. 'Come in and have some tea, Simon.'

Graham leaned forward to speak to Hugh. 'Come to the estate office when you've finished. It's in the east wing, Will can show you. I must get back now.' Standing up, he excused himself to Isobel, 'I've plenty of work to be getting on with', and left the room abruptly.

Anna raised her daintily arched eyebrows in surprise. 'What did I say?'

'Oh, he's got a lot on his mind just now.' Lucy said hastily. 'Simon, have you met Hugh? He's staying in the old farm cottage.'

Simon came further into the room and said, 'Yes, we have met.' The two men nodded politely to each other, as Will muttered something to his grandmother and left the room hurriedly.

'You've met my grandmother,' Lucy went on, and Simon turned to Isobel Rossington with a rueful smile.

'I have, of course, when you came to the pottery with Lucy. I do hope I haven't disrupted your tea too much.'

Isobel was vexed by Anna's presumption, but her annoyance faded before the anxiety in Simon's eyes. 'No, of course you haven't,' she said. 'You know we're always pleased to see you. Sit down and I'll pour you some tea.'

Simon sat down beside Lucy on the sofa. 'That's not entirely true, is it?' he asked quietly. 'I am sorry, but Anna was rather hard to refuse.'

Lucy smiled. 'I know. She always has been. Don't worry about it, it isn't a problem.'

'But it is with Graham, isn't it?' He hesitated a moment, then hurried on, 'Look, Lucy, if it's going to be difficult for you I don't at all mind forgetting about prospecting around here. You've got to work with Graham, and there's enough on your plate just now without having to cope with his resentment too.'

Lucy's smile set. 'No,' she said firmly. 'There's no harm in your detecting and Graham will come round in the end. He's always been besotted with the priory ruins and worried about them being damaged. He'll soon see that you aren't doing any harm.'

Simon still looked doubtful. 'Well,' he began uncertainly, 'if you're sure ...'

'Oh, don't be silly, darling,' Anna broke in, passing her tea plate back to Isobel for another slice of cake. 'Graham's always fusty about those old buildings, but you really don't need to take any notice of him. Lucy can manage him, can't you, Lucy?' She smiled mischievously at her, but went on without waiting for an answer, 'Where are we going to start, Simon?'

Simon leaned forward eagerly. 'Well, I've been working around the lake, but as we're setting out from here I thought we'd work our way down towards it along the brook behind the old scriptorium.'

'Do you know much about the site?' Hugh asked.

Simon turned towards him. 'Well, no, only what we've all picked up from Graham. Most of the villagers know something, from hearing him at one time or another.'

Anna screwed her charming features into an equally charming grimace. 'Don't we just!'

Hugh looked at her, amused. 'I wouldn't have expected you to claim to be a villager.'

She laughed. 'No, perhaps I won't, but I can claim to be a local – by birth, at least,' she added, 'and any contact with

Graham inevitably results in some knowledge of the old priory.'
An expression of surprise crossed her mobile features. 'I can't
believe you haven't found that out already.'

'I'm shortly to have a guided tour,' he replied blandly.

She groaned fatalistically, and then brightened. 'Well, find
out if there's anywhere particularly exciting to look. Isn't there
some story about treasure?' she asked vaguely, turning back to
Simon.

'There always is, but usually without any foundation,' he
said ruefully. He added quickly, as he saw the disappointment
in her face, 'But they had a guesthouse and many of their visitors would have been wealthy, so there's always a chance that
they may have dropped something interesting.'

'Do you expect to find anything in particular?' Hugh asked.

'It's more a question of finding anything at all,' Simon replied
practically. 'The finding of an artefact can be just as interesting
as the discovery of something ostensibly more valuable.'

'I should have thought you would be interested in finding
pottery,' remarked Isobel.

'Well,' he said, 'I enjoy seeing what has been found and getting ideas from the shapes that were used, but searching for the
remains on site requires more archaeological skill than I have.'
He added thoughtfully, 'Besides, although I enjoy my craft very
much, I do also like doing something different at times.'

'I can understand that,' Isobel commented. 'My husband was
such an active man that many people were quite confounded
when he became a bibliophile later in life.'

She smiled at her granddaughter, who was quietly passing
round the refilled cups. 'He particularly enjoyed finding books
for Lucy when she was a little girl. Do you remember *Down on
the Farm*, Lucy?'

'Of course, how could I forget it? He must have regretted it,
when he found he had to read it to me every night for months.
But that wasn't a specially old book, was it?'

'No, dear, but his own interests were in rare editions, as

Hugh has already noticed. '

Hugh nodded as Lucy turned an enquiring gaze on him. 'Yes, indeed, there are some very rare editions here, and many of them are in good condition.'

Lucy looked round at the shelves with a shamefaced air. 'I've never really had a look at them, and I wouldn't know much about them if I did,' she said apologetically. 'They're all Will's now, of course, and maybe he'll have more interest in them than I do.' She turned back to Hugh. 'I'm sure he wouldn't mind you looking through them, if you're interested.'

'I'd like to do that. I've already spotted some old favourites. Do you have a catalogue?'

Lucy looked blank, but Isobel replied immediately, 'Yes. At least, there was one once, because William wrote it himself, although I haven't seen it for many years now.'

'Ask Graham when you see him,' Lucy suggested. 'He's sure to know all about it.'

She turned round as Anna stood up. 'Are you going already?'

'Yes, darling, we must get started while it's still light,' Anna said, glancing expectantly towards Simon, who got to his feet at once. 'You must give me a ring tomorrow, and we'll fix up lunch or something. I need to catch up on all the local gossip and Daddy never knows any of it, bless him, and I want to hear all about your venture. We've scarcely had chance to talk about anything yet.'

She held out her hands to Hugh, who had also risen to his feet, and leaned forward to kiss his cheek. 'Hugh, I'm so glad you're here. I'll call round and we'll arrange to have dinner, and I'll tell you all about the riches we've found.'

He nodded. 'You do that, Anna. I'll look forward to it.'

She bent down to kiss Isobel's cheek. 'Bye, bye, Gran Ross. Thank you for the usual delicious tea. I'll see you again soon, but I promise to cheer Daddy up too.'

With a wave of her hand she left through the French window,

followed by Simon, who bent down to pick up a long sacking-wrapped object which he had left on the terrace.

Hugh looked at Lucy, raising his eyebrow in a way that she already found familiar. 'The instrument of annoyance?' he asked.

She smiled. 'Yes. Thank goodness he didn't bring it in.'

Isobel spoke quietly, 'Graham has been here a very long time, dear. Your father was fond of him and trusted him absolutely. He has the interests of the manor, and of you both, very much at heart, so I think you must try to be tolerant of him.'

She sighed. 'He finds the modern easy-going way of doing things rather strange, and perhaps a little threatening. I'm not sure I don't myself, sometimes.'

Lucy laughed and hugged her. 'Nonsense, Gran, you're in your element. And I do know about Graham, and I wouldn't dream of upsetting him over anything important.' She turned to Hugh. 'In fact, I'll deliver my peace offering in person.' She smiled at him. 'I do hope you won't be very bored.'

For a moment she thought he was not going to smile back, but then he did. 'I'm very sure I won't be,' he said, meeting her eyes steadily.

He turned to Isobel. 'Thank you for the tea. I enjoyed it very much. Are you sure you won't mind if I come to look through the books?'

'Not at all, Hugh,' she replied firmly. 'I shall be very glad if they give you any pleasure, as they did my dear William.'

TWO

The two men halted on the wide unrailed bridge over the brook. 'The prior's lodging was the basis of the Rossington house, and was, as you can see, quite separate from the main monastic buildings over there.' Graham gestured at the buildings on the far side beyond a thicket of overgrown rhododendrons. 'The gateway ahead was his entrance into the cloister, and the doorway underneath the arch still leads into the nave of the church. There's a corresponding doorway on the south side for the villagers to use, and some of them still do.'

He pointed to the left of the gateway. 'See, that was the dorter, facing west, above the scriptorium. The monks used to come into the room above the gateway and down the stairs there for the night services. The room has gone completely, but there are still traces of the night stairs in the corner opposite the church door. The infirmary was in the north-western corner of the cloister garth, at the end of this block, with a warming room near it. You can't see it from here, but there's a small chapter house behind them.'

'The buildings have lasted well,' commented Hugh, surveying what he could see of them.

'Yes, they're not in bad condition, although these bushes are a damned nuisance. They were planted by the Victorian Rossingtons to add a touch of scenic value, I suspect, and we're constantly having to cut the wretched things back from the walls. One day I hope we'll be able to root them all out. Anyway,' Graham returned abruptly to the main topic, 'it was once a wealthy house, so it was kept in good repair until the decades before the Dissolution. You'll see from the size of the granary and barn by the gatehouse just how much grain and straw they expected to store, and there was plenty of animal accommodation as well.'

'What happened to it after the Dissolution?' Hugh asked, looking around.

'We're not entirely sure,' Graham replied. 'The last prior was James of Rydean, and it seems the place had gone to rack and ruin under his rule. The Commissioners' report for the priory shows that there were only six monks here then, when once it was a house of over forty, and on their first visit the Commissioners found these six, including the prior, roaring drunk and disporting themselves with women from the village.'

He shrugged. 'They were far from any supervision here, and it seems that most of the church vessels had been sold off to pay for the riotous living. The land that remained hadn't been farmed, and the house had long lost its reputation for illuminated religious texts.'

He smiled a little regretfully. 'They didn't have a hope when the Commissioners came, and it seems that they ceded the property without any struggle. There's no record of where any of them went or what they did afterwards, although legend has it that James of Rydean hid the remaining priory treasures, intending to return later and retrieve them. But he died within two weeks of the monks' final departure, killed, oddly enough, on the cliffs behind the manor.'

Hugh raised an eyebrow. 'So the prior's treasure lies hidden, waiting for somebody to find it.'

Graham nodded. 'Of course, and over the centuries there have always been people who were sure they knew where and what it was, but somehow it's never been found.'

'I should have thought Mrs Rossington's husband would have been the most likely person to have known the possibilities,' Hugh commented idly.

'Oh? Why him in particular?' Graham sounded puzzled.

'Wasn't he a great bibliophile? If there were any clues, I should have thought he would have stood a good chance of coming across them.'

'Yes, I suppose so, if there were any to be found. In fact, I believe,' Graham went on more slowly, 'that he was particularly interested in books covering the history of the area, and of the monasteries, but then if he'd found any clues he'd have done something about it.' He added reflectively, 'We don't even know what the treasure was supposed to be, and in the end I don't think William really believed it existed. There are similar rumours attached to almost every historical building.'

'Do you believe in it?' Hugh asked.

'The treasure?' Graham looked at him quizzically. 'Seriously, I can't say that I do, although Francis Rossington and I spent many hours searching for it when we were younger. There can't be a stone in the place that we haven't lifted or pressed, or a hole that we haven't excavated hopefully.' He smiled wryly. 'It's a story that has a particular appeal when you're young.'

'How about Lucy and Will then? Do they believe in it?'

'I wouldn't know, to be honest. They've neither of them been much interested in the old priory; growing up with it, they've just taken it for granted, although Will was always interested in the proper monastic names of the old rooms.' He hesitated for a moment and then continued, 'Francis was a bit like that too; I was always more fascinated by it and the old stories about it than he was. He preferred scrambling about on the moors and the cliffs, and the children have taken after him. It must be hereditary, I suppose,' he added, 'because Francis can hardly ever have taken them with him. He wasn't a bad father, you know, it was just that he couldn't seem to stay here after Johanna died.'

He was silent, gazing back into the past, but he looked round as Hugh said softly, 'But Will and Lucy are both sufficiently interested to not even consider selling their inheritance.'

Graham did not demur, but nodded with some amusement. 'Oh, scratch the surface and they're both true Rossingtons. It was Harry Rossington who bought the priory from Henry VIII, with money the family believes he made from buccaneering. He paid a paltry sum for it as it was so far from any major highway – and the king was probably in need of funds again. The place had been deserted, except for the odd vagrant, for over ten years after it was ceded to the Crown, and the Rossingtons built it up into their home, the base to which they've all returned time and again. I could never see one of the family giving it up.'

They had been moving on slowly as they talked, through the ruined arch of the prior's gateway into the cobbled yard which had once been the green garth of the cloisters. Here and there broken masonry and truncated stumps protruded through the jumble of farm equipment, indicating all that remained of the pillars which had supported the roof over the cloisters. Weathered and crumbling arches still lined some of the aisles where the monks had walked on the worn paving slabs, and occasional partitions showed the site of the carrels, where they had sat in fine weather to delineate their elaborate letters and fantastic beasts. Although the buildings now housed cattle during the winter, both the inner and outer walls were in good repair, in spite of the sea breezes that came through the window apertures which had once been roughly glazed and shuttered.

Graham was frowning now. 'I sometimes wonder if vagrants are using it again,' he said meditatively, looking about the garth.

'Why?' Hugh asked, startled.

'Oh, nothing really,' Graham said. 'I've found a cigarette stub, and spent matches from time to time, and none of us smoke. But just a feeling,' he said slowly, 'that somebody's been here.'

'Possibly walkers sleeping here overnight,' Hugh said. 'The coastal path must bring a few through the village, and I know the pub doesn't let rooms. There's nowhere else for them to stay, is there?' He looked enquiringly at Graham.

'No, not that I know of. Maybe that's it,' the other man replied, unconvinced. He added, 'Don't mention it up at the house, I don't want to worry them.'

Hugh was about to query this, but Graham turned to the church, opening the north-west door and beckoning him in. 'It was reconsecrated for the villagers to use, but as you can see,' Graham said, 'there has been precious little done to it. Lack of money,' he added succinctly. 'The Rossingtons have kept it in repair over the centuries, but could never bring themselves to spend more on it than was absolutely necessary. Every penny they had went on their ships, their animals and their lands, and probably in that order too.'

The interior of the small church was whitewashed and plain, with narrow windows filled with clear glass. Through these could be seen silver-lichened oak branches, their ancient limbs washed with fresh green spring growth and swaying lightly in the evening breeze. Simple wooden benches stood on the stone floor, and in the tiny chancel a small oak cross spread its arms widely against the violet-studded grass bank that was visible through the east window.

Hugh stood on the worn flagstones by the door and looked about him silently, absorbing the sense of peace and serenity that emanated from the little building. He turned eventually to Graham, who waited patiently beside him, and said quietly, 'You're very lucky. It could have been completely spoiled by the Victorians. As it is, it's untouched and quite perfect.'

Graham nodded, pleased, but said, 'Yet you'd be surprised how often people are disappointed.'

'Anna?' Hugh queried in disbelief, unsure why he should think first of her.

'No, oddly enough I think Anna rather likes coming here,'

Graham said, a little taken aback himself. 'When she's at home she sometimes helps Lucy do the flowers.' He pointed at the vases of daffodils and pussy willow in the window recesses. 'But that woman, Tilly what's-her-name, is always on about brightening the place up. "But, Lucy, sweetie, the place is so dull", that's her all over.' He shrugged and went back out of the door, pausing outside, 'Look, you can see where the night stairs came down. The edges of the steps are still visible against the wall.'

He indicated the blocks of rubble nearby. 'All the better stuff was carted away over the centuries when the cottages on the estate were built. Most of the older ones have some stones from here. Look in the east wall of yours and you'll find a gargoyle showing quite clearly.' He preceded Hugh into the cloister garth again and pointed up at the eaves of the dorter. 'It came from up there and has fellows here and on the outside, too. But they're all getting loose, now,' he sighed, 'and I must try and get something done about them before long.'

Hugh glanced up briefly, but continued to walk along the old flags of the cloister peering at the walls of the carrels and in the scriptorium. Graham watched him for a while and then asked curiously, 'What are you looking for?'

'Signs of the book cupboards. Where did they store their work?' Hugh asked, swinging round.

Graham looked at him thoughtfully. 'Not many people think of that,' he said. 'I've never found any sign of cupboards, so I can only think they used wooden chests and cupboards, perhaps in the scriptorium itself.' He gestured around. 'It may have been a question of space.'

Hugh nodded, but did not look entirely satisfied. 'Mmm, I suppose so.' He strolled along the northern walk, peering into the infirmary and the warming room, which now contained the debris of the hay and straw that had been stored in them.

Graham leaned over his shoulder at the entrance to the warming room and pointed into the gloomy interior. 'There are a couple of good fireplaces, but that's all that's left in here

now.' He glanced about disparagingly. 'All of this muck will be
cleared out in a couple of weeks. Come and have a closer look
then, if you're interested.'

'I'll do that,' Hugh said. He crossed the garth, treading with
care over the slippery cobbles, and went into the entrance courtyard. He stood looking around, and when Graham joined him
he pointed to the large building on the south side. 'What was
that?'

'The guesthouse,' Graham replied, watching his face and
catching the surprise in it. 'Yes, it was large for the size of the
foundation. I wonder if people lodged here, waiting for a boat
across to Brittany perhaps, and no doubt the patrons of the
scriptorium would have visited too.'

'Wouldn't they have lodged with the prior?' Hugh asked
abstractedly, measuring the size of the guesthouse with his eyes.

'Usually that would be the case,' Graham agreed, 'though
our original prior's lodging was quite small, so they probably
dined with him, but slept here.' He looked at the building too,
and pointed to the west end. 'There are only bare walls inside
of course, but there's a small room at the end, with a door into
the chancel.'

'A sacristy?' Hugh asked in amazement.

'I wonder that myself.' Graham looked around. 'It'll be dark
soon, but when you come again I'll show you inside. In the
meantime come and see this. I think it's rather a fine example.'
He led the way eagerly past the gatehouse to the northern side
of the courtyard, and Hugh saw finely sculptured arches sheltering a stone trough set into the wall of the building.

'A lavatorium!' he exclaimed, and ran his fingers lightly over
the arches. 'Yes, it is a fine one. And is the frater behind?'

Graham nodded. 'And the kitchen next door, with yet
another fireplace. The frater has the remains of a pulpit halfway
up the wall, so the brothers must have enjoyed readings while
they ate.'

Hugh was silent for a while, looking shrewdly at the stone

walls. 'I think you're right, you know. It must have been a wealthy house at one time,' he said. 'Have there ever been any excavations?'

'Man, who'd want to excavate here, at the back of beyond?'

Hugh considered him in surprise. 'I think you'd find quite a few people who'd be very interested. After all, the site has hardly been disturbed at all, and I should think it's pretty well unknown.'

'Would they do much damage?' Graham asked, rubbing his chin thoughtfully.

'Good Lord, I should hope not. They'll have to remove the soil and debris very carefully because they could find all sorts of things in it. Even tiny fragments of pottery could be important.'

'But we wouldn't be able to use the buildings if people were digging on the site, would we?'

'Do you use them all year round?' Hugh asked.

Graham shook his head. 'No, mainly in the autumn and winter.'

'Well, I should think that would be ideal. Most excavations are done in the spring and summer months, I think, but I'm pretty sure that any archaeologist would be only too keen to fit in with your times.'

Graham did not say anything, but stood in the courtyard looking around. Hugh waited for a while and then said 'I've got a contact in that field. Would you like me to get him to ring you to discuss it? I really know very little about it, and he could explain it all much better. And of course he could tell you whether an excavation would be at all feasible.'

Graham hesitated, and then he shrugged his shoulders. 'Well, why not? I'd like to know more about the place, and I can discuss it with the family when I know exactly what would be involved.'

'And you know,' Hugh sounded enthusiastic as he went on, 'the excavations and any finds would be quite a draw for visitors – an added attraction along with Mrs Rossington's teas.'

Graham frowned. 'I'm not so sure about that. People tramping all over the place are a damned nuisance. Like that potter from the village,' he carried on sharply. 'We never know where he's going to be or what he's going to be doing.'

'Do you know anything about him?' Hugh asked.

'Oh, he's been here for a few years, and I've never heard anything against him. He's a pleasant enough chap, I suppose,' Graham replied reluctantly, continuing with a disparaging note in his voice, 'although I can't imagine how he earns a living from making pots.' He did not see Hugh hide a smile. 'It's nothing about him in particular, it's just that he'll be the tip of the iceberg. Because Lucy's let him loose in the grounds there'll be other fools who want to jump on the bandwagon, and before we know where we are there'll be idiots underfoot everywhere.' He sighed irritably and then looked apologetically at Hugh. 'I'm sorry, it's not your concern. It's just that there's enough to cope with without this too.'

'Well,' Hugh offered, 'at least if you admit paying visitors to the site you can outline the boundaries very clearly. That would contain most of them.'

Graham was silent for a minute, ruminating, and then he smiled cynically. 'Well, if we've got to have fools underfoot we might as well have ones who pay for the privilege, so there might be something in this idea of yours. God knows,' he said heavily, 'we could do with the money.'

'If it worked, you know, you could take it even further.' Hugh smiled at the questioning look Graham gave him. 'Well, you've got the old guesthouse and refectory. Why not return them to their original use? Bed and breakfast, and possibly longer-term accommodation in some of the other buildings, with the option to self-cater or to eat in the same place as the monks.' He caught himself up with a grin. 'I could always write your publicity details.'

Graham laughed. 'Is that what you do? I should imagine you could sell most things.'

'I've never really tried. It's the place and all its possibilities – the ideas just come bubbling up.'

'It's alright having them,' Graham said, sobering quickly, 'but the trouble is, those sort of ideas cost a lot to put into practice, apart from any other consideration. And there isn't the cash to spare here for new ideas. All that we've got is already spoken for by the estate, and,' he added grimly, 'that isn't enough.'

'Mmm, it is a problem,' Hugh said pensively. 'But I should think you would be eligible for a grant or two from the various heritage bodies. It would be something to look into.'

'Perhaps.' Graham was noncommittal. 'Still, you've certainly given me plenty to think about. I'll see what I can find out, and maybe call a family conclave to discuss it, if it looks at all possible.'

Hugh realised that the matter was closed, and returned to the tour by asking, 'What about the stews? I imagine the brook runs from the lake – was that where they were?'

'Yes, there were two big stews, formed by the separate damming of the two brooks which run through that part of the grounds. They were made into one large lake in the eighteenth century, when a fair amount of planting was done around the priory buildings. It was the beginning of the few attempts by the Rossingtons to make the ruins picturesque, but thank God they were all far too practical to take off the roofs or demolish any of the walls.'

'You can be thankful they didn't try their hand at renovation, either,' Hugh said dryly. 'That could have been just as harmful.'

By now they had come out of the gatehouse and were admiring the great barn which lay to the south of the rutted track, and the granary which lay to the north. Hugh looked with particular appreciation at the latter, a two-storey stone building, its roof slates patched with yellow and bronze lichens. Then his gaze passed beyond it to the lake, just visible through banks of the ubiquitous rhododendrons. He staggered suddenly as something large and solid hit him neatly behind the knees.

Recovering his balance he looked down to see Hades standing on the rough turf, his mouth split in a wide grin and his pink tongue lolling out between his gleaming teeth. 'Will won't be far away,' Graham remarked as Hugh bent to stroke the dog.

'I'm not,' Will said, emerging from the rhododendron thicket. 'There's a group of whacking great carp over there.' He pointed vaguely to one corner of the lake.

'Are you a fisherman, Will?' Hugh asked, straight-faced.

Will glanced at him suspiciously and then grinned. 'Well, they were at least this big,' he said, stretching his hands out and considering them before spreading them even further.

'Maybe you should bring a rod down,' Hugh suggested, but Graham snorted.

'They're wily old brutes. Probably the same ones Francis and I used to fish for.' He looked over towards the lake and then straightened his shoulders. 'I'd better be getting back. There's some work I want to finish before it gets too late.' He said to Hugh, 'Come round any time you like. I'll be thinking about what you said.'

A shout reached them, and they turned to see a man striding purposefully over the turf towards them. A well-built man in his late twenties, with thick carefully controlled black hair curling onto the collar of his turquoise linen shirt.

'Somebody for you?' asked Hugh, thinking the newcomer looked familiar.

'I'm not expecting anybody,' Graham said, and then his voice deepened in surprise. 'Good heavens. Jack!'

The man had reached them now, and clapped Graham heartily on the shoulder. 'Hello, Uncle Graham. I thought I should find you here.' He glanced down at his black trousers, immaculate from waist to knee, then wet and rumpled below, and said grumpily, 'I thought I'd take a short cut, but I forgot about the damned brook.'

'Jack,' repeated Graham, obviously pleased, but just as obvi-

ously surprised. 'What on earth are you doing here?' He added
sharply, 'There's nothing wrong is there?'

'No, no,' the younger man assured him. 'I was passing
through, and thought you might put me up for a few nights.'
He scowled. 'I'd have rung you, but I can't get mobile reception
down here.'

'Of course,' Graham assured him. 'I'm just on my way
back now. Oh,' he remembered Hugh and Will, standing silent
and curious nearby. 'Hugh, this is my nephew Jack, my sister's son.' He looked at Jack. 'And maybe you remember Will
Rossington?'

Jack smiled perfunctorily. 'Not really, you've grown a lot, of
course, Will.'

He glanced at Hugh, who nodded amiably and asked
politely, 'Are you working nearby?'

'No, just touring,' Jack said abruptly. 'Excuse me if I don't
hang around, I'd like to get out of these.' He gestured at his
trousers, and then slapped Graham on the back. 'Come on,
uncle, let's get back.'

Hugh and Will stood watching the two men walk briskly
down the track towards the lodge, the younger talking animat-
edly, the elder somewhat stiff and hunched.

'Well,' Will said, astonished, 'I didn't even know he had a
nephew. What a laugh, I wish I'd seen him fall in the brook.'
He added, 'You know, I think Graham still minds about Dad.
Being dead, I mean.'

Hugh chose his words carefully. 'When you grow up closely
with someone, you miss a great deal of your own past when
they die.'

'Yes, I suppose so,' Will said doubtfully. 'Of course, he knew
Dad much better than I did, I didn't really know him at all.' He
dismissed the matter from his mind. 'What did you say to him?'

'What?' Hugh lost the thread of the conversation momen-
tarily. 'Oh, about the priory buildings.'

Will grunted dismissively. 'Was it very dull?' He did not

wait for an answer, but went on quickly, 'Look, come to the far
end wall of the old granary.' He led Hugh eagerly a little way
up the track, and pointed. 'See that arch, it was built for owls
to use, so they'd keep down the rats and mice. I'm sure there's
a barn owl roosting there now. I've seen him hunting at dusk,
and I hear him at night when he screeches.' He sniggered. 'I bet
I could make Anna believe it's a ghost.' His amusement faded
quickly and he added with a note of dismay in his voice, 'Oh
Lord, here she comes again.'

'Then now's your chance,' Hugh said, laughing. 'Anna,
Will's just been telling me about a ghost.'

Will scowled, and Anna said sympathetically. 'Hugh can be
a brute.' She turned to Hugh and chided him, 'It's nothing to
laugh about. Why shouldn't there be a ghost here? Enough has
happened in this spot, in all truth.' She looked at Will. 'Have
you ever seen it? Do you think it could be the last prior? Isn't he
supposed to come to look for his treasure?' Will was speechless,
but Anna carried on enthusiastically, 'We should have a ghost-
spotting evening before I leave. That'll be such fun! Will, do tell
Lucy.'

Will nodded and muttered something before stalking off
round the priory. Anna watched him go and turned to Hugh, a
hint of laughter in her eyes. 'I don't seem to go down too well,
do I?' she asked ruefully.

Hugh grinned. 'He's not old enough to appreciate your finer
points, Anna. Not yet.'

She smiled and said, 'I'm not sure the day will ever come.'

'Well, you can try out your charms on a more susceptible
male,' Hugh promised her. 'Graham has just had a surprise visit
from his nephew, who sounds as though he'll be around for a
bit.'

'Oh,' Anna was interested, but puzzled. 'I didn't even know
he had a nephew. What's he like?'

'Very carefully turned out,' Hugh said succinctly. 'Jack ...'
He broke off as Anna gasped, and looked at her curiously.

'Oh, lumme,' she said inelegantly. 'Yes, I've heard of him. He came down years ago and Lucy hated him. He was always playing horrible little jokes on her, and being so astonished that she didn't think they were funny.' Her brows drew together. 'I certainly don't get the impression that he's a diligent nephew.' She looked soberly at Hugh. 'I wonder what he wants.'

Hugh nodded. 'Mmm, I wondered too. Will clearly didn't know him, so I guessed he couldn't be a regular visitor.'

Anna was reminded of their earlier conversation. 'Hugh,' she rebuked him, 'it really wasn't nice of you to tease Will about the ghost. I know it was probably an owl or something like that, but he may take the idea quite seriously.' Her last words were lost as Hugh put his arms round her and hugged her, shaking with silent laughter. Her eyes narrowed as she considered him. 'I don't suppose you're going to let me in on the joke?'

He shook his head, releasing her. 'Anna, you're a source of endless pleasure.'

She was amused. 'That seems to be a nice way of saying I'm dim.'

Hugh looked at her glowing face. 'Come on, Anna, nobody could ever think you were dim, unless you meant them to. Not even down here.' He paused and then asked curiously, 'Why are you really here? Filial duty also seems an unusual role.'

'It is,' she confessed. 'But I haven't seen Daddy for a bit, and,' she went on frankly, 'I'm hoping to persuade him to fund a trip to Paris.' Hugh looked at her enquiringly and she confided, 'Blanchard Rey will be auditioning soon for parts in his new play. He's dramatised *The Queen's Necklace*, you know, and I would give quite a lot to play the part of Jeanne de Lamotte Valois.'

'The villainess, wasn't she?' Hugh queried, having only a hazy recollection of the story and its connection with Marie-Antoinette.

'Yes, it would be a very interesting part,' Anna was unusually serious, but suddenly her eyes sparkled. 'It seems a shame to go all that way, though, and not spend some time in the place, doesn't it?'

'Your reasoning is impeccable,' Hugh assured her. 'Is your father amenable to the idea?'

'Well, not yet,' she admitted, 'but he likes having me to stay, and after a few days he'll listen to what I'm saying.'

'So you're having to work at it,' he remarked.

'No need,' she said sweetly, 'he's actually open to reason, and it is reasonable for me to stay there until the final choices are made.'

Hugh studied her thoughtfully. 'You're sure of the part,' he commented.

'No,' she shook her head instantly, 'I'm not, but I know I would be good for it, and my French is okay, one of the benefits of having a French mother. I should be well in the running,' she corrected herself, 'am well in the running.' She smiled at him. 'Strictly between ourselves, I'm auditioning fairly soon.'

'I see.' He was amused and, unexpectedly, impressed.

'But in the meantime,' she dropped her seriousness and spoke gaily again, 'we must find ways of amusing ourselves here. Maybe we should cultivate Jack.' She slanted a look at him as a thought struck her. 'But what are you doing down here? It's the last place I'd have expected to bump into you.'

He shrugged. 'Unlike you, I got tired of town and decided to get out. I'm trying my hand at a bit of writing, a bit of photography.'

She stared at him in astonishment. 'But Hugh, how strange. It doesn't seem in the least like you.' Then she laughed. 'But then I'm not sure, you've always been rather unfathomable.' She eyed him doubtfully. 'I suppose you're not having me on, are you?'

He smiled mockingly. 'Not this time, Anna. Isn't that what you're doing with the potter?'

Diverted, she smiled but shook her head reprovingly. 'No, of course I'm not. He's not seriously interested in me, and I'm only relying on him to relieve any possible boredom.' She reflected for a moment. 'But I'm not sure this scanning, or whatever it is, will do.' She made a wry face. 'The poor dear is very earnest about it, you know. He gets excited about the most ghastly bits of bent metal.'

'What were they?' Hugh enquired, interested.

'Oh, I don't know. Little muddy strips of metal in the shrubbery, and then a whole heap of bent rusty rods near the lake. They didn't look like anything to me, but Simon said they were possibly parts of an old fish trap.' She looked appalled. 'He's seeing if he can find any more, but I thought it was time I got back to change for dinner. It's awfully messy round there.' She held out one daintily-shod foot for him to see the mud caked on it.

'My poor Anna,' he laughed as he leaned forward to kiss her lightly on the cheek. 'I should hurry away before you have to put the pieces together.'

'God,' she sounded horrified, 'what a frightful prospect!' She glanced over her shoulder. 'Yes, I'm off, but do come and see me soon, Hugh.' She waved to him as she made her way back towards the priory buildings.

Hugh stood for a while where she had left him, and then he began to follow the faint path that wound in and out of the bushes around the lake. The sun was low on the horizon and where the shrubs grew high and close together it was already gloomy. He emerged suddenly into a more open stretch of ground and saw Simon beneath a group of silver birch saplings that were swaying gently in the light breeze.

He was bending, absorbed, over a small pile of metal, his fair hair catching the last of the evening light in a halo effect. Just beyond him the brook poured smoothly out of the lake and flowed serenely along its course around the priory buildings. Hugh walked soft-footed over the grass and said, 'Hello.'

Simon jumped, and turned sharply. 'Hello, I didn't hear you coming.'

'Too engrossed,' Hugh said, pointing at the tangle of metal. 'Anna said you'd found a fish trap.' There was a note of query in his voice.

Simon grinned. 'Poor Anna, I'm afraid it wasn't the sort of thing she was expecting.' He looked down at the collection on the grass. 'I think it may be a fish trap, but I'm not sure yet. Do you know anything about these things?'

'I've never seen one before. What makes you think that's what it is?'

'Well, look,' Simon crouched down and pointed to various pieces of rusty metal in the heap. 'Do you see, if you put these together like this they begin to form a sort of cage?'

'Mmm, yes, I see what you mean,' Hugh said, studying the structure carefully. 'Why would it be here, though?'

'Well,' Simon explained eagerly, 'this would probably have been a good spot to place one, here where the brook leaves the lake, and I expect this one got chucked on one side if it was damaged. Or,' he added, 'it may just have been left when the monks were turned out.'

'It sounds plausible,' Hugh admitted. 'Why don't you ask Graham? He's likely to have more idea about it than anyone else.'

Simon flushed. 'Yes, you're right, of course.' He hesitated and then carried on bluntly, 'But, to tell the truth, I'm not in particularly good odour with him at the moment. He disapproves of this quite fanatically.' He gestured toward the metal detector which lay under the silver birches.

'If you can show him something you've found that belonged to the priory, you might win him over,' Hugh suggested.

Simon considered this and his face brightened. 'You could be right. I'll give it a go. Lucy's been so good about backing me that I'd like to ease the situation a bit for her sake.'

Hugh looked around and said, 'Surely you won't find much more tonight? It's getting quite dark.'

'Oh, detecting isn't a problem in the dark, but,' he grinned, 'digging can be. I'll call it a day. Are you going home now?' When Hugh nodded, he said, 'I'll walk along with you. Lucy won't be expecting me back, and I think she wants to finish off her signboards.'

'How do you think her tea business will go?' Hugh asked as the two men threaded their way through the bushes.

Simon smiled broadly. 'Knowing Lucy, I think it's bound to go well. I can't think of anything she couldn't do well if she put her mind to it.' He glanced at Hugh, who nodded silently in agreement.

'What's she doing about the advertising, do you know?'

Simon brushed some mud from his fingers as he answered. 'Well, that's the problem, of course. She's well off the beaten track here, but she's advertising wherever she can. Posters in the tourist information offices and entries in their promotions, as well as the big boards for the main coast road. Tilly did the illustrations, and I gather they look pretty good.'

He laughed out loud as he saw the fleeting expression that crossed Hugh's face. 'She's a decent artist, you know, if you steer her away from the quaint little animals and cute little children. And there's even a market for those. But Lucy worked out what she wanted and Tilly painted the pictures. I haven't seen any of them, but I believe Lucy's pleased with the results. Anyway, I think people will come out of curiosity at first; it'll be slow of course, but there's nowhere else at all decent to offer any kind of competition.'

'I'm sure you're right,' Hugh said. 'You must have some experience in that area yourself.'

'Oh?' Simon sounded surprised, and glanced enquiringly at Hugh. They had by now emerged onto the farm track beyond the granary and were nearing the fork that led to the village past Hugh's cottage. Twilight had already deepened and there was an opaque darkness under the oaks that grew protectively around the farmhouse.

'I was thinking of the pottery.' Hugh explained. 'You're off the usual tourist route as well.'

'Oh yes, but my main customers aren't tourists. You could say that I'm a service industry,' Simon said. 'I supply most of the local hotels and guesthouses with crockery and bits – you know, jugs, vases, ornamental plates, that sort of thing. They display my card, and the larger places generally put on an exhibition of work in the main season. Just occasionally,' he added deprecatingly, 'I do have a studio full of people who've come out specially to look at the goods and see how they're made.'

'Does it pay?' Hugh enquired bluntly.

Simon did not seem at all offended. 'I'll never be rich from it,' he answered blithely, 'but I pay my bills and have something left over to live on.' He turned the tables neatly. 'Are you in the rat race, or thinking of opting out yourself?'

'Not thinking of,' Hugh was unforthcoming. 'I have opted out.'

'Oh?'

'Yes.' Conscious perhaps that this sounded rather bald, Hugh expanded his statement. 'I have several commissions for photographs, and some for articles.'

Simon was clearly interested. 'That's pretty good. What sort of things?'

'A mixture really. Subjects I'm interested in, like wildlife and local history.' Now that he had warmed up Hugh seemed keen to talk. 'I think the priory may be worth investigating. Very little seems to have been done about it.'

'How do you mean?' Simon asked, puzzled.

'Well, from talking to Graham it seems that no archaeological research has been done on the place at all. So it has some interesting potential.'

'I see.' He did not really sound as though he did. 'Do you think it's sufficiently interesting to make a dig worthwhile?'

Hugh nodded. 'I'm pretty certain it would be.' By now they had reached the gate to his cottage, where they paused and Hugh turned to Simon. 'Come in for a beer,' he invited. 'I've got some bottles chilling in the fridge.'

Simon hesitated. 'Thanks, I'd like a drink, but I should really finish some pots. I've almost got a kiln full of work and I want to do a firing soon.' Then he said, 'Yes, go on, I'll just have a quick one.'

They went up the crooked path together and Hugh fished a key out of his pocket to unlock the door. He opened it onto the soft darkness of a small hall and flicked a switch to turn on a tiny overhead light which just relieved the blackness. He led Simon through the door on the left into the sitting room and switched on a couple of lamps. 'Make yourself comfortable,' he said. 'I'll just get the fire going and then I'll fetch the drinks.'

He picked up a matchbox from the table and bent over the ready-laid fire in the grate. He struck a match and applied the tiny flame to the paper, standing back to see if it was catching. It flared into life around the wood so he went back into the hall and across into the kitchen on the far side.

When he reappeared carrying two tankards of foaming beer he was pleased to see the fire was burning well. Simon had seated himself in a worn velour-covered armchair near it and was watching the flames with mesmerised interest. He looked up as Hugh put the tankards down on the table. 'Thanks. I was looking forward to this.'

Hugh had just seated himself in the armchair opposite when they heard a knocking on the front door. 'Are you expecting visitors?' Simon asked.

'No,' Hugh replied, getting up again and going through to the hall. From his chair in the sitting room Simon heard and recognised the light breathless voice that greeted Hugh as he opened the door. His mouth twisted and he picked up his tankard, sipping slowly at the beer.

'Simon, sweetie! How lovely! I didn't expect to see you here! I had no idea you two were such friends.' She paused for breath and Simon, who had put down his tankard and risen to his feet, smiled pleasantly at her.

'Hello, Tilly. Have you come to join us?'

'Oh no, no, I wouldn't dream of interrupting you. I only came for a quick word with Hugh, but it's fortunate that you're here too.'

She sank back into the chair Hugh had been using and took a glass of gin and tonic from him as he came through from the kitchen. 'How sweet of you. I do just love a teensy drink of gin every now and again.'

Simon glanced at Hugh's impassive face as he pulled up another chair, and then sat down again himself, looking across at Tilly. She was a woman of medium height, and was running to plumpness in spite of sporadic attempts to hinder the process. She had a fondness for bright elementary clothes, which were generally baggy but somehow always seemed to cling in all the wrong places. They overwhelmed the faded blonde curls which floated wispily around her head. She was prone to twist these girlishly as she talked, in spite of the fact that she was well on into her thirties.

Neither of the men had spoken but Tilly did not notice this as she rushed back into speech. 'I've just come from the manor; I was anxious to see how Lucy was getting on with the signs. She's finished them, but I'm afraid they're a bit dull, really.'

'These are the ones you painted, are they?' Simon interrupted.

She pouted. 'Yes, I painted them, after all work's work, isn't it? But Lucy was very insistent about the pictures and really, of course, she knows what she wants, but people aren't going to find them at all interesting. Not at all, you know.' She had been waving her thin hands about as she spoke and Simon found himself watching her glass, waiting to see how soon she would knock it over.

He dragged his gaze back to her face with an effort. 'Just what did you paint in the end?'

'Oh,' she shrugged petulantly. 'A beastly red teapot and a smaller picture of the manor house. So boring.' She finished her drink and sat back in the chair, looking like a multi-coloured bird in her long cotton skirt and bright purple blouse. She twisted a curl round one finger and smiled smugly.

'But it's a good job I went. I caught up with Anna,' Tilly glanced sideways at Hugh, a speculative gleam in her eyes, 'and when we got to the house she started spouting about ghost hunts. I must say I was surprised she could think of something like that, and of course Lucy would have dismissed the idea at once if I hadn't been there. She's a sweet girl, but really I don't think she's got a sensitive bone in her body.'

She drew a breath and rattled on, 'Anyway, I think it's such a clever thing to do and I was sure you'd both want to take part. Lucy clearly didn't want to be bothered with it so I've said I'll arrange it. It's not all that convenient because I've got simply masses to do at the moment, but I really couldn't let such an opportunity pass.'

She paused and picked up her glass, gazing at it thoughtfully when she found it was empty. Hugh made no move to refill it and she twirled it carelessly between her fingers. 'Two weeks time, on Saturday, I thought that would be good. It'll give us time to make arrangements.'

'What arrangements?' Simon asked guardedly.

'Well, sweetie,' she stared at him, astonished, 'but of course we need to do some investigations, research you know, about what we might see. Everyone knows the story of the last prior, but in a place like this there must have been lots more incidents that have left their mark on the timeless warp.'

Hugh's mouth twitched suddenly but Tilly carried on, wrapped up in her ideas. 'I don't just mean tragedies, of course, although I'm afraid most ghosts do walk because of the terrible way their lives ended. But I personally believe that any kind of strong emotion leaves traces, and that people who had been involved in great love affairs are just as likely to return to the scenes of their happiness. And all those ruthless Elizabethans must have been tremendous lovers.' She paused, her eyes unfocussed as she gazed wistfully back into the past, and Simon studiously avoided looking across at Hugh.

It was Hugh who broke the silence. 'I seem to be the only person who doesn't know the story of the last prior. Where does he haunt?'

'Why, the priory, of course,' Tilly said.

'Wouldn't you expect it to be the place where he died?' Hugh asked curiously.

'Well, no, of course not, Hugh,' Tilly leaned forward as she spoke. 'Surely you can see that he'd revisit the place that he'd been turned out of so brutally? It must be such a strong reason for him to return.'

Simon sensed Hugh's scepticism and interrupted, 'The story is that the prior and the monks return each year on the anniversary of their expulsion and resume their activities in their old home.'

'Well,' Tilly said doubtfully, 'that's more or less what I'd heard, but I thought they came back because of that last monk who was buried so hurriedly.' Hugh raised an eyebrow and she rushed to explain, 'I think one of the monks died just before they were all forced to leave, and they didn't have time to bury him in the monks' graveyard, so they left his body in the crypt.'

She frowned, twisting one of her curls absently. 'And I suppose if they hadn't buried him with all the proper rites they'd be afraid that he wouldn't rest in peace or something, so on the anniversary of his death they come back and try to finish the job.' She stiffened suddenly. 'But of course, we must get Lucy to have the crypt opened and have the remains committed properly, and then his spirit will be able to rest quietly.'

Simon intervened again. 'But then you won't see your ghosts.' Tilly looked across at him, indecision written over her face. 'When are the monks supposed to return?' he asked.

'That's just it, I believe it's usually in a couple of weeks, that's why I thought it would be best to have our expedition about then.' She brightened. 'Of course we could carry on with that, and then get Lucy to see about the crypt and the burial and everything afterwards.'

Hugh resisted the urge to ask why it was not the unfortunately buried monk who haunted his resting place, but with commendable patience enquired instead, 'Was this what you wanted to see me about, Tilly?'

She started and turned to him, the tip of her tongue just moistening her thin lips. 'Hugh, sweetie, no, it wasn't just that. I particularly wanted to ask you a tiny favour.' She did not appear to notice his unresponsive silence. 'It's a result of doing all this painting for Lucy. I suggested she have little animals and birds scattered over her signs, examples of the local wildlife, you know. But she wasn't very keen, which is her loss, but then people who aren't artistic do find it so difficult to use their imagination. Anyway, I thought it was an idea I could use myself.'

She slanted a wide smile at Simon. 'I thought if Simon would kindly let me have some of his plates I could paint them,' she returned her plaintive gaze to Hugh, 'and I was just wondering if you had some books I could look through. About birds, because it's so important to get the details right. Of course, I know that you'll probably need to use them yourself, so I wouldn't want to take them away. I thought maybe it would be easier if I just pop up here from time to time and look through them.'

Simon turned abruptly towards the fire, lifting his tankard to his lips to drain the last of his beer. Hugh looked at Tilly thoughtfully. 'There are a couple of books that may be useful to you,' he said slowly, 'but I don't have them at the moment.' He ignored her attempt to speak and carried on blandly, 'My reference books wouldn't be much help to you, but I think I can sort out something.'

She smiled at him, twisting her curls furiously. 'That's so sweet of you, Hugh. I promise not to get in your way.'

'Don't worry about that. A friend is probably coming to stay with me in the next couple of days and I'll get him to bring the

right books down with him. I shan't need to use them, so you
can borrow them for as long as you want.'

'Oh,' she was nonplussed. 'That's very kind of you, but,' she
rallied, 'I wouldn't want you to go to all that trouble.'

'It's no trouble,' Hugh said firmly, and turned as Simon put
his tankard down on the table and got to his feet. Their eyes
met briefly. 'Do you need to get back?'

'Yes, I'm afraid so. Thanks for the drink. Call in on me when
you're in the village.'

'Sweetie, if you're going home I'll come with you,' Tilly said,
putting her own glass down. 'I don't really like walking down
the lane in the dark, it's just a little bit creepy.'

'Then how are you going to manage your ghost hunt?'
Simon demanded as they went out into the hall.

'Oh, that's different,' she said, smiling archly at Hugh as he
held the front door open. 'You'll both be there and I'll feel perfectly safe.'

With a little wave of her hand she preceded Simon down the
twisting path, stumbling once or twice and clutching his arm.
At the gate she turned and waved again, blowing a kiss to Hugh
as he stood in the doorway.

Once they were safely out in the lane Hugh closed the door.
He took the empty glasses out into the kitchen and poured himself another drink, then carried it back into the sitting room and
sat down in an armchair, stretching his legs out in front of him.
He sipped at his beer and gazed thoughtfully at the fire, which
was now burning merrily.

After a few minutes he leaned forward and placed a couple
of logs carefully in the grate, and then drew the telephone across
the table towards him. He dialled a number and waited for the
response. When it came he parried a number of exuberant que-
ries and finally spoke at some length. The voice at the other end
asked some questions sharply, which Hugh seemed to answer
satisfactorily. He swallowed some more beer and said, 'I think
it may be a good thing, but see what you think. And play it

easily – don't push too hard.'

A bellow of laughter greeted his warning and Hugh, who was about to put the receiver down, suddenly remembered something. 'And look here, can you bring me down a couple of bird books with good pictures? Yes, it's urgent and no, I'm not explaining now why I want more of them. It's a matter of self-preservation.'

Another roar of laughter came down the line, the mocking note clearly audible, and Hugh, with a brief word of farewell, ended the call.

THREE

'Hugh, how fortunate! I've been wondering if you'd forgotten about me.' Anna smiled enchantingly at Hugh.

He smiled back at her, saying lightly, 'I can't imagine ever doing that, Anna.' He glanced round the village street, where the brook burbled cheerfully down its stone channel between rows of low crooked cottages. 'Is this the closest you can come to shopping in the metropolis?'

She gurgled with laughter. 'It is at the moment. This,' she waved her rush basket under his nose, 'is tonight's dinner. I collected it from the fish van – Daddy loves Dover sole.'

His eyes gleamed with amusement. 'The dutiful daughter's deed for the day?'

She sparkled at him. 'Yes, indeed it is. And now I'm going to call in on Simon for coffee.'

'I hear my name,' Simon's voice said, and he appeared in the doorway of the tiny village shop behind them. 'And I can tell you're on the scrounge for coffee, Anna, and even,' he waved a packet of chocolate digestives at her, 'ready to raid my biscuits.'

'Simon, how yummy. I adore chocolate biscuits,' she responded happily.

'I'd better go and pay for them then, or Mrs Hamble will think I'm absconding with them.' There was a sound of expostulation from the shop's interior, and he turned towards it with a smile, saying over his shoulder, 'You both go and get the coffee on, and I'll be with you as soon as I've finished here.'

Anna looked at Hugh appealingly. 'You will come, won't you?'

'Yes, of course. I haven't been to the pottery yet.' He took her arm and they walked down the pavement past little gardens bright with daffodils and wallflowers until they reached Simon's rambling cottage near the harbour. Hugh stood outside for a while looking at it, noting the whitewashed walls covered with rambling roses and honeysuckle, each now putting out fresh green shoots. The roof folded protectively over the tiny upper windows, which were almost hidden by the jasmine that grew profusely up from beside the front door. One end of it had been the wheelwright's shop and stood back from the main frontage, although it had now clearly been absorbed into the cottage.

Anna, fed up with waiting, had gone indoors and could be heard filling a kettle. She had left the front door open and Hugh went through it and down a shallow step directly into the sitting room.

He looked around with interest. The sepia-washed walls and ceiling complemented the wooden beams, and the oak table and brightly patterned throws draping the armchairs contributed to a general aura of simplicity. He strolled over to the table and flicked through a pile of magazines, before turning to look at the books stacked haphazardly on the shelves under the windows.

Anna came to the kitchen door. 'Come and see the pottery,' she commanded. He followed her into the kitchen, briefly taking in its spartan brightness as they walked to the back door. The rambling garden was centred on a huge gnarled apple tree, studded with lime-green clusters of mistletoe. A variety of shrubs crowded the borders, encroaching on a rickety wooden garden bench and table. Just visible at the bottom of the garden was a small brick outbuilding, whose dusty windows were partly obscured by a huge buddleia, which was already thrusting out vigorous new growth.

'I don't think Simon's much of a gardener,' Anna said doubt-fully. 'It's never very neat, but he says he prefers it like this.'

'And so do my customers,' Simon observed from behind them. 'It creates a very cottagey impression, with almost no effort involved.' He grinned at Hugh. 'I sometimes think Anna has a hankering for Victorian-style bedding plants.'

Anna eyed him dubiously. 'I don't know much about gardening, but this does look awfully messy.'

'It's supposed to,' he assured her. 'Never mind, come into the pottery.'

He opened the door and ushered them into an open-plan interior, with tables and benches displaying the finished items near the doorway. Beyond, Simon's working area was dominated by his wheel and firing kiln, which were surrounded by stacked shelves supporting an assortment of mugs, plates and bowls waiting for firing.

Simon stood back and let them wander about. Hugh picked up the fatly rounded mugs, enjoying the feel of them in his hands. Most of the finished ware was in a rich terracotta colour, highlighted here and there with a scattering of creamy yellow pieces. Hugh looked up, cradling a plump mug. 'Dunley school?' he asked.

Simon was surprised. 'You do know your stuff, don't you?'

Hugh smiled deprecatingly. 'Oh, I only know a little about a lot of things, so it's easy to sound knowledgeable.'

'Well, you're right. I learned my craft at Corrington.' He put out a finger to touch one of the bowls lightly. 'I've always loved these colours and shapes.'

Hugh put the mug down reluctantly. 'They are very satisfying.'

It was Simon's turn to smile. 'I hope so.'

Hugh turned to go, and then swung back abruptly. 'Look, I like these,' he said, picking up the mug again. 'Could you let me have a set of twelve in the yellow?'

'Sure.' Simon gestured into the back section. 'There's a couple of dozen waiting for the next firing. I'll probably do it tonight, and you can have your twelve out of those.'

Anna had drifted away through the garden some time ago, and they could hear her voice calling that coffee was ready. They went back across the garden and Hugh asked, 'Do you never lock the pottery?'

'Nobody locks anything around here. There's never a problem,' Simon said easily.

Hugh smiled wryly. 'It's difficult to comprehend that when you're used to living in London.'

Two steaming mugs of coffee stood on the kitchen table, so they picked them up and took them through to the sitting room where Anna was comfortably settled in one of the armchairs with a plate of chocolate biscuits beside her. She looked up from the magazine she was reading and said, 'I was afraid I'd have to finish these off by myself.' With conscious generosity she passed the plate to Hugh, who had seated himself in one of the other chairs.

Simon leaned over to take a biscuit, and settled back onto the sofa, demolishing the digestive in two quick bites before saying to Hugh, 'You seem to have stirred things up at the manor.'

Anna sat up, dropping her magazine into her lap, while Hugh looked blankly at Simon. 'I have? How?'

'That awful man!' Anna exclaimed. Hugh glanced at her in astonishment before looking back at Simon, raising a questioning eyebrow.

'I went up yesterday to look for some more of those lead tags that Lucy was so pleased with. Plant tags,' he explained, seeing that Hugh had not understood. 'It'll help her to know what the original shrubs were, apart from the rhododendrons. Anyway,' he continued, 'they were all in a ferment because of some chap who was visiting Graham. He'd come about the old priory, and said you'd sent him.' He looked enquiringly at Hugh.

Hugh nodded, his expression grim. 'Mike Shannon. He's one of the leading experts in the archaeology of that period. He seemed interested when I told him about the place, but I wasn't expecting him to come down so quickly.'

'Well, he went over virtually every inch of the place with Graham and appeared to be even more interested when they'd finished. I think he's supposed to be coming down again to spend more time looking around.'

'I hope they don't let him talk them into something they'll regret,' Anna said with some asperity, and again Hugh stared at her in surprise. She met his eyes, flushing delicately. 'He's so bossy. And he's the rudest man I've ever met.' Her hands clenched involuntarily. 'I can't imagine how they could want to have him around for any length of time. And,' she looked reproachfully at Hugh, 'I simply can't see how he can be a friend of yours.'

'He's not as bad as he seems,' Hugh offered placatingly, wondering what on earth Mike could have done to offend Anna, whose temperament was generally equable and sunny.

'Huh!' She snorted in disbelief. 'What's he interested in the place for anyway?'

'Excavation, I should think, which might lead to some form of restoration?' Hugh raised an eyebrow and glanced at Simon, who agreed. 'Yes, it sounded like it. Graham seemed quite cock-a-hoop about it all.'

He saw Anna's expression out of the corner of his eye, and grinned. 'The family, of course, were exuberant, and all sorts of ideas were being tossed around. I'm surprised you haven't heard about it,' he said to Hugh, who shrugged.

'I was in Coombhaven yesterday. Will knew that. I expect I'll see him today.'

'Wouldn't your expert let you know?' Simon asked curiously.

Hugh laughed. 'Mike? He won't get in touch until he wants a bed.'

'Well, maybe he won't come back,' Anna said hopefully, and adroitly changed the subject. 'Next time you go into town, you might let me know.' She pulled a wry face. 'The Landrover's okay locally, but I have to borrow Daddy's car if I want to go any distance, and he always seems to need it himself.'

'Never mind, Anna,' Simon said in a consoling tone. 'I'll probably have to take some pots from this new firing in during the next few days. I'll give you a ring and you can come too if you're free.'

Her face lit up. 'That would be lovely. It's such fun wandering around the streets watching the tourists, and I could go down to the harbour.'

'Do you get many tourists here?' Hugh asked idly.

Simon shook his head. 'Not really. But we're getting more walkers, so I wonder if the area's in one of the walking guides. I believe Tilly does an unofficial kind of bed and breakfast sometimes.' He added, 'The pub has good beer but doesn't do food, so it really only pulls the regulars in, thank God, and the odd beer enthusiast turns up once in a while.'

'There's not really much here for tourists,' Anna explained. 'It's a bit off the beaten track, and has no famous attractions.'

'What, no old smugglers' routes?' Hugh teased.

'Oh, everywhere near the coast has got those,' Anna responded. 'We used to sneak into the old caves in Rosgully Cove and look for tunnels. We weren't supposed to, of course,' she added ruefully. 'The tide comes in very quickly along that part of the coast. In fact,' she said slowly, as a memory came back to her, 'that's where one of Jack's little jokes on Lucy was nearly fatal.'

'What did he do, trap her in them?' Hugh demanded.

'Oh, nothing that serious.' she said soberly. 'Anyway, she wouldn't have taken him there, I think she avoided him like the plague.' She glanced round at Simon, then at Hugh again. 'He just altered her watch to make her late for lunch, and of course she came out of the cave to find the tide already round the promontories.'

'How did she get out?' Hugh asked quietly.

'She climbed up the cliff face and got home late for lunch, with her jeans torn and her hands bloody. Of course Mr Rossington guessed where she'd been, so there was an awful row.'

Anna smiled at Hugh. 'I'll show you where they are if you like, but they're best seen from the sea.' She looked at Simon. 'Do you know if old Bob is still hiring out his boat? I haven't been sailing for ages.'

'Yes, I think so,' Simon said. 'He certainly was last summer. If he is, why don't I fix a day with him and we can all go out for a trip?' He glanced enquiringly at Hugh, who nodded in agreement. 'Do you think Lucy would like to go too?' he asked Anna.

'Of course she would. She's a very good sailor, we used to go out a lot together in Bob's boat during the holidays. I tell you what,' she said, 'we'll have to arrange something for before the Easter holidays or else Lucy probably won't be able to come.'

Hugh stood up, stretching his back. 'That seems like a good idea. Let me know the date.'

'I will,' Anna said, 'but don't say too much about it. We don't want Jack coming too.' She smiled at them engagingly. 'He's a bit of a pain.' Her brows drew together. 'I really don't know why he's hanging around, he's obviously bored out of his mind.'

'So our man from the City hasn't made a good impression,' Simon quizzed her. He added, 'The locals don't like him either, in spite of the rounds he buys in the pub.'

Hugh looked down at Anna curled up in her chair. 'Is he bothering Lucy?'

'Have you ever seen a stiff glittering icicle impersonating a very pretty girl?' Anna asked. 'No, Jack's not bothering Lucy.'

Hugh's lips twitched. 'I almost find it in me to feel sorry for the man.' He turned to Simon. 'I ought to be off. There's work I should be doing while the weather stays fine.' He bent over

Anna, kissing her cheek. 'Come and have dinner with me this evening?'

Her eyes sparkled with pleasure. 'I'd love to. Do you know somewhere nice to go?'

'Yes. Wait and see!' He smiled at her. 'I'll pick you up at seven.' He raised a hand to Simon and let himself out of the cottage, walking swiftly back up the street towards his own place.

He had opened the garden gate before he saw the figure standing irresolutely by his front door. 'Hello, Will. Have you been waiting long?'

Will turned thankfully. 'No, not really. I was just wondering where to look for you.' Hades had come round the corner of the cottage from the back garden, with his ears pricked at the sound of his master's voice. At the sight of Hugh he gave a delighted bark and bounded eagerly down the path, jumping up to give his face a welcoming lick. Hugh pushed him down gently and wiped his face with his sleeve. 'Hello, Hades, good boy. No, down!' he said sharply, stroking the excited dog who was pressing against his leg.

Will rushed on, 'There's been masses happening at home and Mike Shannon says you told him to come.' He looked expectantly at Hugh, who grinned.

'So I did, but I didn't think he'd be quite so quick off the mark. Look, come in while I pack up some gear and a bit of food. I'm going over to the tern colony – do you want to come with me and tell me what's been going on?'

Will acquiesced gladly and was soon busy slapping ham between thickly buttered doorsteps of bread. Hades lay beside the table, watching him alertly and swiftly disposing of any pieces of food that fell onto the floor. Hugh looked over at them as he was putting his camera equipment and sketching things into a canvas bag, and smiled at the sight of lunch.

Will felt the glance and looked up, saying defensively, 'I like thick slices, don't you?'

'I always like something I can get my teeth into,' Hugh

responded affably.

Five minutes later they had left the cottage and were walking below the arching branches of the trees in the ancient sunken lane that skirted the village. Hades trotted ahead of them, his long tail swinging happily and his nose twitching as various scents assailed it. Will needed no encouragement to start his story and it came brimming out as soon as they were in the hidden lane. 'Mike's fantastic, isn't he? He raved about the old priory buildings. He thinks an excavation would be interesting, as there's been so little disturbance to the site. And he says that we'd probably be eligible for grants and things for restoring and converting the buildings.'

He broke off, calling Hades over to disentangle a bramble from the dog's long tail, and then resumed his narrative. 'He just carried everyone along with him, even Graham, and I don't think he was altogether happy about it at first.' He frowned. 'I thought Lucy was rather annoyed as well, but I expect she was a bit taken aback by Mike.' He smiled ruefully. 'She was soon full of ideas, of course. She's talking about renting accommodation and things like that, and Graham said you'd suggested the same sort of thing. Do you think it's possible?' he demanded suddenly.

'Would you mind, Will?' Hugh asked. The boy was silent for a while as they turned onto a track between high blackthorn hedges, whose newly opening buds were draping the bare branches with a lacy green haze. Hades snuffled hopefully under the bushes – there were rabbits around here, and rats as well, and he was always keen to catch one, or even two.

'Yes, I would,' Will said meditatively. 'I don't really like the thought of people all over the place, but,' he sighed and then straightened his shoulders, 'I think it may mean the difference between keeping the house and grounds or building on the land, and I'd hate to do that.'

Hugh saw a momentary trace of the Rossington ancestors who had built up the estate in the immature features of the boy beside him. He waited to see what else Will had to say, and after a short pause the boy continued, 'So it seems to me that it might be the only answer. I didn't really think Lucy's tea scheme would be enough, but she'd never think of giving up.' He looked at Hugh, who was thinking how like his sister he was. 'There's so much to be done, you see, and not enough money, and on top of that death duties were rather high.' He broke off to call Hades, who was trying to squeeze through a narrow gap into the field beyond, and then returned to his original question. 'Do you think letting rooms would work?'

Hugh was slow to reply and picked his words carefully. 'Yes, I do think it could work, but it would be a long-term project. You'd have the excavations and the recording of the finds, you'd have to follow the grants application procedures, and then the restorations and conversions would probably have to be done with authentic materials by expert craftsmen. It would all be very time-consuming. Would you be able to hang on that long?' he finished bluntly.

'We'll hang on,' Will said simply. 'Mike says we can charge people to go round the excavations, and Gran thinks she'll be able to do lunches as well as teas. Lucy's wondering if we can squeeze people into the house for bed and breakfast. She thinks she can use my room when I've gone back to school, but she can't.' He looked up at Hugh with determination hardening his face. 'I'm not going to go back to Gudwal's. If we don't have to pay the fees we'll save more than Lucy could earn while I was away, and there's no reason why I shouldn't go to the local school. I can't see that I'll learn anything different.'

'Have you discussed it with them yet?' Hugh enquired noncommittally.

'No, I've only just made up my mind, but I expect they'll fuss.' His tone became outraged. 'They're all planning ways to make money, but in the end it's my responsibility and I should make the biggest contribution. I can't do much yet but I can save on those stupid fees, and if I'm here in the evenings and at the weekends I'll be able to help. And,' he added naively, 'I want to be here if Mike finds anything. Do you think he will?'

'Mike is a pretty good judge of an interesting site,' Hugh replied. 'But he'll be thinking in terms of archaeological finds, you know, things that will give him some idea of how the monks lived and worked here, rather than treasure.'

'Oh yes, I know that.' Will was scornful. 'I've never believed that old story anyway. Gran says that tales about treasure and hidden passages and hauntings and all that rot always grow up about old buildings. But do you think he'll find bones and things?'

Hugh considered. 'Well, the monks must have had their own burial ground in the precinct. Do you know where it was?'

Will shook his head. 'No, I've never thought about it. Wow, so there should be some bodies then,' he said excitedly.

'Mmm, I should be inclined to think so,' Hugh replied cautiously, wondering what Lucy was going to think about Will's new interest.

'Wow,' Will said again, and then remembered something. 'Oh Lord, have you heard what Tilly's after now? She wants us to find the bones of the last monk and give him a decent burial. It's only another of those old stories, but she'd believe anything. Still,' he said regretfully, 'it could have been interesting. Maybe,' he added, brightening up, 'Mike'll find that body. Wouldn't that be something?'

'I think it might,' Hugh commented dryly. 'What did Lucy say about this?'

Will grinned. 'She said that it didn't seem like a good time just now, but she'd think about it. Tilly didn't like that at all, but Lucy won't be pushed around. Tilly went off in a bit of a huff,' he said with satisfaction, ending scornfully, 'her and her ghosts!'

He smiled wickedly. 'She fancies Jack, you know. Serves him right. He tried it on with Lucy but she hates him. She said he was a really nasty boy when she saw him before and he hasn't changed at all.' He frowned. 'I hope he doesn't stay much longer. Gran says we're not to be rude to him because of Graham.' He added thoughtfully, 'But I don't think Graham likes him much either so I guess it's harder on him.'

He fell silent for a while, and then glanced a little shyly at Hugh. 'Tilly said,' he hesitated, and then hurried on, 'she said you fancy Anna, that she saw you together.' He looked up anxiously at Hugh, whose lips were twitching. 'Do you?'

'Will, we're good friends,' Hugh replied, wondering where Tilly had been lurking. 'You don't always have to fancy women, you can just like them.'

Will sighed with relief. 'Good.' Then he added, unwittingly wiping away Hugh's amusement, 'I told Lucy you didn't.'

By this time they were emerging from the track onto the shingle at the top of a sloping beach, and Hades scrambled eagerly over the pebbles onto the sandy expanse beyond. The tide was just beginning to come in and Hugh eyed it expertly. 'There's time to get round the headland, but we'll have to stay there until the tide turns again or come back up the cliff path.'

Hades took a few tentative steps towards the water and looked pleadingly at his master. Will turned apologetically to Hugh. 'I think I'll go for a swim. I don't feel as though I could keep still right now, there's so much to think about.'

'That's fine. You please yourself,' Hugh replied amiably.

'I might come over the cliff path later, though,' Will added pensively.

'I'll save you some food, just in case,' Hugh promised, and waved a hand to them as he set off over the firm sand to the jutting eastern headland. As he reached it he looked back in time to see Will's naked figure splashing into the curling waves, with Hades leaping ecstatically around him.

Little rippling wavelets foamed up to Hugh's feet as he rounded the headland. He did not immediately pick his way up the beach towards the nesting area where terns were flying in and out purposefully. Instead he looked up at the bulky granite cliff beside him, eyes narrowed. Suddenly he saw a dark narrow cleft that interested him, but rather than scramble up he stood back and assessed the huge seal-grey and rosy pink boulders piled haphazardly below it.

He walked up the beach, staying beside the cliff, and put his rucksack down well above the high water mark. Then he turned back, assessing the cliff above him as he went. When he stood below the cleft he looked around quickly, before picking his way carefully up over the tumbled boulders.

A short time later he stopped and bent over a rusty metal stake which had been driven into one of the dark grey boulders. He moved on again and soon scrambled onto a flat lip of granite in front of the cleft, where he paused, looking around once more. Seeing no one in sight, he slipped a small torch out of his pocket and stepped through the cleft into a cave.

Although it was narrow it was also high, and after he had taken a few cautious steps it opened out into a large circular space. The granite floor was uneven but quite dry, so that he was sure the sea did not come up this far. The sides sloped steeply upwards and he shone the beam of his torch around them, playing it backwards and forwards for a while until he finally let it rest on a spot high up on the back wall.

Hugh picked his way up the wall, testing his foot and hand holds before moving, his torch clenched firmly in his left hand, and found the climb quite easy. He reached a bulging outcrop of rock just below the cave roof and leaned against it, shining his torch behind it. Grunting with satisfaction, he pulled himself up and into the shadowy darkness beyond. Just as he stood up cautiously the light of his torch shone on something small and white on the ground and he bent down to pick up a cigarette stub. He considered it pensively for a while and then dropped it.

Glancing at the luminous hands of his watch he hesitated, wondering whether to follow the passageway any further. He shone the torch light further into the blackness, noting that the narrow tunnel slanted gradually upwards, and then came to a decision.

He found his way carefully back down the cave wall and, turning off the torch, walked confidently across the rock floor to the narrow sliver of light at the entrance. When he stepped out onto the rock lip the brightness dazzled him for a few seconds, then he scanned the upper part of the beach and the far headland. The cove below was hidden from view by a lumpy fist of rock and it was only as he slid round it that he saw a figure on the lower beach.

Hugh hesitated, keeping well back, and then recognised Will. His brows drew together for a second, then he continued to pick his way carefully downwards. His foot dislodged a stone and he swore quietly as it fell rattling down in front of him.

Will looked up and waved. 'Hi!' he said, approaching as Hugh jumped down onto the sand. 'I wondered where you were.' He glanced up at the cliff and then grinned at Hugh. 'Were you exploring the cave?'

Hugh nodded. 'I used to do some caving and I couldn't resist it. Have you been up there?'

'Of course,' Will said. 'I should think every local kid has been. It's supposed to be one of the smugglers' hideaways, but I reckon they wouldn't have stored the stuff here, they'd want to get it away as quickly as possible. Don't you think so?' he demanded.

'I'm sure they would,' Hugh agreed, and asked guilelessly, 'Are you hungry yet?'

'You bet,' Will replied, turning back up the beach, followed thoughtfully by Hugh.

Hugh leaned back in his chair, curling his fingers round his coffee cup. Anna sipped daintily at her Benedictine and smiled across at him, while his eyes ran over her appreciatively. She was a startlingly exotic picture. Her flame-red dress outlined her figure perfectly and her dark hair curled buoyantly on her shoulders. One slender foot swung gently to the rhythm of the music, played softly by a quartet on a small dais at the end of the room.

'Lucy and I used to come here as children. It's odd to see it now,' she reflected, looking round admiringly at the white walls and brightly patterned curtains. Near their table a wooden waterwheel turned slowly and silently, safely encased in glass, and above their heads thick beams supported a high open ceiling. 'It was clever of you to find it.'

'What was it like then?' Hugh enquired idly.

'Oh, a bit of a dump really. It was still a working mill, you know. I used to like watching the grain pouring out of the chute into the sacks, but Lucy was always fascinated by the wheel turning. She nearly fell in once and there was a terrible fuss.' Anna sipped her drink and carried on, 'It was worked by an old man who'd been the miller for years. He used to let us ride up on the pulleys,' she smiled reminiscently. 'His wife had been dead for ages and the place was falling down around his ears, but he wouldn't move out. He said the mill was his life, but I believe he was taken to a home in the end.'

'Did you mind?' Hugh asked softly and she paused, her thoughts turning back.

'No, I don't think I did, I don't think I really thought about it at all, although Lucy was in a terrible rage over it. But,' she said pensively, 'I mind now. Silly, I suppose. But I'm glad it hasn't been spoiled. Who owns it, do you know?'

Hugh shook his head, and she smiled. 'Oh, well, it doesn't matter. Daddy always knows who owns what and where. They've done a good job on it though.' Her expression changed abruptly as she looked over his shoulder. 'Oh no,' she exclaimed in tones of heartfelt horror, 'Jack's just come in.' She added in surprise, 'He's got somebody with him. No,' she said sharply, 'don't look round.' She peered carefully into the far corner where Jack had been seated. 'Oh dear, it's Philly Leygar.'

She suddenly smiled brilliantly at Hugh and said urgently, 'Quickly, talk to me, he's coming over.'

Jack loomed over Hugh's shoulder, beaming broadly, while the young woman behind him hung back, her frank open face troubled. 'Well, what a lucky man I am tonight. I've just brought young Philly here for a treat, so dire for the poor girl stuck down on the farm all the time with the yokels. Mind if we join you?' He reached out for a chair as Hugh turned to face him.

'Jack, what a splendid thought.' He heard Anna's slight indrawn breath. 'But,' he said firmly, 'not tonight. Anna and I have a lot of catching up to do.'

Anna smiled enchantingly at Hugh and reached across the table to touch his hand lightly with her own. Jack drew away from the chair slowly, his face darkening. 'Fine,' he said shortly. 'We wouldn't want to interrupt.' He took Philly by the arm and turned her towards the table in the corner, his back rigid with anger.

'Oh dear,' Anna said again. 'I wonder if I should have a word with Philly.'

Hugh shook his head. 'She didn't look particularly happy with him. I should leave her to think about it for herself.' He added thoughtfully, 'It may be dull down here for her, so she might find him interesting.'

'Huh!' Anna looked disbelieving. 'With his stories about money-making in the City? She's a bright girl, you know.'

'I'm sure,' Hugh said, and enquired, 'Is that what he does?'

Anna shrugged. 'I don't know, I don't think he actually said what he does.' She reflected. 'Probably something very junior, don't you think? He's so full of himself that he'd definitely go into details if he really did anything important.' Hugh glanced at her, struck once again by her perspicacity.

'But I think,' she added suddenly, 'he said his father deals in antiques, so maybe he's involved with that. Anyway,' her face lightened, 'we won't let him spoil our evening.' A thought struck her. 'I wonder if Lucy knows about this place? Maybe we should bring her and Simon one evening.' Hugh frowned, and she asked with an inflection of surprise in her voice, 'Why ever not? Don't you like them?'

'I think the boot may be on the other foot.' Hugh answered slowly. 'I suspect Lucy may not be altogether pleased with my interference at the priory.'

'Don't be silly, Hugh,' Anna admonished. 'Lucy has never liked being told what to do, but although she may flare up when she gets into a temper she's eminently reasonable when she cools down again.'

'I hope so,' he said evenly and held out his hand as she put her glass down. 'Let's dance.' She stood up gracefully and allowed him to lead her onto the small dance floor. She leaned close to him as they circled skilfully, her bright skirt swirling tantalisingly around her legs. 'We must do this more often,' she murmured in his ear.

'Yes, you're a splendid dancer, Anna. You would be wasted here for any length of time.'

Her body stiffened against his in momentary anger before relaxing into the steps again. 'So your precious friend thinks. He clearly doesn't believe I have a brain in my head because I'm not interested in a pile of mouldy old stones.'

'Mike?' he queried, and she nodded abruptly.

'You don't want to take any notice of him. He doesn't have much interest in anything if they aren't mouldy old stones,' Hugh said consolingly.

'Well, he was interested enough in Lucy,' she snapped, 'but then she does own the mouldy old stones.' He forbore to correct her, judging the moment to be inauspicious, but she suddenly pulled a rueful face. 'I'm becoming a harpy. Never mind, I can live without red-haired bores.'

'That's probably just as well,' Hugh said levelly. 'I can't imagine any woman, even you, competing successfully with mouldy old stones in Mike's life.'

'Is that a challenge?' she asked, lifting her chin haughtily.

'A friendly warning, if you like,' he replied bluntly.

Her eyes narrowed as she considered him, then she laughed lightly. 'Well, should I ever be tempted I'll bear the warning in mind, but how fortunate that I've generally got other fish to fry.'

'There's always the flounder in the corner,' Hugh said smoothly.

She gave a mock shudder. 'But I can't bear men who wear velvet jackets and look after their hair more carefully than I do.'

Hugh drew them to a halt beside the musicians as the music ended. He spoke briefly to the leader, who nodded and swung into a lively jive.

'Darling, how lovely!' Anna's face glowed with pleasure as she stepped expertly to the tune and twirled flamboyantly under Hugh's arm. Oblivious to the admiring, and occasionally envious, glances from the other diners, and the lowering black glares from Jack at his corner table, they dominated the dance floor until the music ended.

Leading a radiant Anna back to their table Hugh offered her another drink, but she glanced down at her wristwatch and gave a little scream. 'Oh Lord, look at the time. It's after eleven.'

Hugh stared at her in amazement and as she caught sight of his face she gurgled with laughter. 'Darling, it's alright, really it is. I'm quite well, but there was a lot of muttering this evening about gallivanting around and late hours and all the rest of it. The poor dear seems to feel he's not seeing enough of me, although heaven knows I'm there most of the time. Still, I said I'd be back in good time, so we really ought to leave if you can bear to and then I'll stand a chance of being home by midnight. I might even be in time to sit with him while he has his bedtime drink.'

'Cocoa?' Hugh queried, straight-faced, as he summoned the waiter.

Anna shook her head. 'No, no, whisky. He swears he can't

sleep without it. I'm afraid,' she said, letting him put her black velvet wrap around her shoulders, 'you won't be able to come in and have one too, my poor pet. Daddy has very strong views about regular hours and all that.'

They walked across the grass towards his car, and he murmured, 'That must cramp your style a little.'

'Well, not really,' she smiled sweetly, 'and it's so good for me to get my beauty sleep.'

He held open the door of his silver-grey Audi while she got in, and said, 'Not much chance of that when you get to Paris, I suppose, so it must be worth building up your reserves now.'

'Exactly. At least I hope there won't be much chance to sleep a lot – what a waste of Paris!'

He switched on the ignition and turned the car out onto the drive. 'Have you swung it yet?' he asked.

'Well, not yet, but it takes time and patience, you know.'

'I can imagine,' his tone was dry. 'Somehow I didn't think you had a lot of either.'

Her voice was serene. 'Oh, I manage if I want something badly. And really, you know, it's a bit of a game. Daddy will always let me have what I want in the end, but he doesn't like to give in too easily.'

'Why not?' Hugh asked, interested.

'Well,' she considered this, 'I suppose it's partly his character, and partly because he disapproves in some ways of me being an actress. Not quite proper, I suppose,' she said with her beguiling smile. 'But I think he has a sneaking pride in what I've done, although he'd rather die than admit it.' She shrugged. 'Anyway, he'd like to meet you, I've told him all about you.'

She looked mischievous as she saw Hugh glance at her apprehensively. 'Would you like to come to dinner one day next week? I thought it would be fun to ask the Rossingtons too.'

He turned slightly and smiled at her. 'Yes, I'd like that. I'm free any evening, so let me know which is best for the others.'

The moon was nearly full and the elegant Queen Anne house

shone in unearthly beauty as Hugh drew his car to a halt at the foot of the front steps. Anna leaned across and kissed him lightly. 'Don't get out, darling, and thank you so much for the evening. I'll be in touch about next week.'

She slid out of the car as she finished speaking and ran quickly up the stone steps. She put her key in the lock and opened the door before turning to wave as Hugh swung the car round the front circle and back onto the drive.

He drove back at a leisurely pace through the narrow winding lanes, his headlights occasionally pinpointing startled creatures as they went about their nocturnal activities. A barn owl perched on a five-barred gate, head cocked alert for any small sound, and huge eyes gleaming in the light. A couple of rabbits munched busily on the grass verge beneath one of the high hedges, and there was a shiver of movement as a stalking fox slunk quickly out of sight.

When he got back to the village he drove down to the harbour, which was quiet now. Only a single light showed here in the pub, where the landlord was probably clearing up, or, Hugh thought cynically, entertaining a few choice friends. Moonlight cast a gleaming path over the water, but this was obscured from time to time by scudding clouds.

He drummed his fingers meditatively on the steering wheel, then turned and drove back up the street, where most of the cottages were dark. The majority of the occupants had to be up early in the morning and there were few incentives to keep them up late at night. Simon's kitchen light shone like a solitary beacon in the blackness of the street, and as he passed the fuchsia hedge in front of the cottage Hugh caught a fugitive gleam from the pottery.

He turned into the farm lane and paused outside his own cottage for a second, looking about, before pulling into the parking space beside the building. He got out and shut the car door quietly, standing for a while in the vast silence, adjusting to the moonlit darkness until he found that he could see almost as well as if it were daylight. Then he moved quickly up the path to his front door.

Once inside the cottage Hugh pulled off his shoes and ran upstairs, where he quickly changed into his worn brown trousers and pulled on a thick dark jumper. Back downstairs he pushed his feet into stouter shoes and opened the front door again.

He had just reached the gate when he heard the telephone ringing in his sitting room. He hesitated and then turned, walking swiftly back up the twisting path to the front door, his rubber-soled shoes making no noise in the waiting night.

Hugh was awoken the next morning by a loud hammering on his front door. He lay for a minute wondering what the noise was, and then sat up and swung his legs over the edge of the bed. He pulled on a towelling robe as he walked to the bedroom door, and tied the belt as he ran down the stairs. He ran his fingers through his hair as he threw the front door open.

'Will!' he exclaimed in surprise. The boy's face was flushed and he was panting as if he had been running hard. 'What is it? What's wrong?' As he spoke Hugh put his hand on the boy's arm and drew him into the room.

Will caught his breath and spoke with an effort. 'It's Graham. He's been hurt,' he gulped, 'hurt badly. They've taken him to hospital in Corrington, and they don't seem to think it was an accident,' he finished baldly.

'Jesus!' Hugh ran his hand through his hair again. 'Look, come into the kitchen and let's have some coffee. You'd better tell me exactly what's happened.' He half-filled the kettle and put instant coffee into two mugs. He pushed the boy onto a chair. 'Now start at the beginning and take it slowly.'

Will nodded. 'I wanted to talk to him first thing, so I went over to see him. He always starts work early, and I wanted to catch him before he began.'

'You went to the estate office?' Hugh queried, pouring hot

water onto the coffee and adding milk.

'No,' Will sounded impatient, absently accepting the mug that Hugh gave him. 'I went to the lodge, down the drive at the village gates, where he lives. But he wasn't there, so I thought I'd missed him …'

Hugh interrupted sharply. 'What did Jack have to say?'

Will looked at him blankly. 'He wasn't around. We're not sure if he's gone away or not.' He carried on, 'Anyway, I came back to the estate office. Graham wasn't there either, so I was a bit stumped.' He swallowed a mouthful of the hot coffee and pulled a face.

'But the office was open?' Hugh asked, pushing the sugar bowl across to Will.

'It's never locked,' Will said. 'Who'd want to take anything?' He took two spoonfuls of sugar and stirred them slowly into his coffee. Hugh shrugged, and Will brushed the idea aside. 'I was a bit surprised, because even if he's going out he still normally comes to the office first. He says it's the best time to get through the paperwork.'

'What time was this?' Hugh demanded.

'About quarter past seven, I suppose,' Will replied promptly.

'What makes you so sure?' Hugh asked him in surprise.

Will's face was strangely stern. 'I wasn't sure, but I worked it out when the police asked me.'

Hugh raised an eyebrow. 'Okay. Don't skip the running order. What did you do then?'

'Well, I thought I'd look in the diary and see if he was going to be in during the morning. He leaves it on the desk so we can always find him if we need him urgently.'

'And you did?' Hugh put the question in a neutral tone.

'Yes, I did,' Will was blunt. 'I wanted to get him to support me over the school business, before I speak to Lucy and Gran. After all, he is one of my trustees.' He gulped down some more coffee. 'Anyway, there wasn't anything in the diary and I couldn't remember that he'd said something about today in

particular, so I didn't really know what to do next.' He stared
out of the window for a moment, and then glanced at Hugh. 'I
mean, I wanted to get on and tell Gran and Lucy, but I'd kind
of counted on having Graham on my side.'

'You're so sure he would be?' Hugh asked curiously.

'Oh, yes,' Will was quite confident. 'After all it'll save money,
won't it? He's always keen on ways of doing that. Anyhow, I
wandered about a bit, trying to think of where else he could be
and what I should do. I'd got as far as the prior's bridge when I
saw him. At least,' he corrected himself carefully, 'I saw a shoe,
and a foot in it, so I looked in the bushes. Graham was lying
there with blood all over his head.' Will's face was pale, his few
freckles standing out noticeably, and he cradled the mug gratefully in his hands.

'There was one of those big corbel stones beside him and I
thought it must have fallen and hit him,' he carried on slowly,
'so I ran back and got Lucy, while Gran rang up Dr Bishop. He
only lives just outside the village and he hadn't gone to his sur-
gery so he came pretty quickly, but he said we couldn't move
Graham.' Will looked very sober. 'The ambulance came then,
and the police. Dr Bishop had told Gran to ring for them.
They've taken Graham away to Corrington. They carried him
to the ambulance on a stretcher and he didn't move or speak.
Dr Bishop told Gran his condition is critical.'

He stared bleakly at Hugh across the table. 'I'm sure
he thinks Graham is going to die.' His voice wavered and he
blinked hard. He stared down at his mug, holding it tightly with
both hands to prevent them from shaking. 'He hadn't just gone
out, you know. The doctor said he'd been lying there for several
hours, and his coat was wet with dew.'

'What had he been doing?' Hugh asked.

'The police wanted to know that too, but how can we tell?
He must have gone there while it was still dark, you see.' He
looked up from his mug and stared across at Hugh. 'They've
taken the stone away and they've cordoned off the whole of

the priory buildings. They've even left two policemen there to make sure nobody goes into them. Hugh, they must think that somebody hit Graham on purpose,' he swallowed hard, his eyes enormous in his thin face, 'that somebody tried to kill him.'

'It does look rather like that, but they may just be taking precautions,' Hugh replied guardedly. 'The set-up sounds a bit odd, but there may be a natural explanation.'

'I think there must be. I just can't think of one, but why would anyone want to hurt Graham?' Will sounded completely puzzled. 'They've told us not to go away, you know, because they want to ask us more questions, but they've already asked us lots and I can't see what else we can tell them.'

'What are you doing here then, if the police told you not to go away?' Hugh demanded.

The colour flooded into Will's face and he looked slightly abashed. 'Well, this isn't really away and, anyhow, nobody saw me come. I crossed the brook by the lake.' He looked at Hugh appealingly. 'I thought you might come up to the house and help us.'

Hugh stared at him, frowning. 'Will, I can't butt in just like that.'

'Oh, you wouldn't be,' he said eagerly. 'We'd be really glad if you were there. At least,' he amended conscientiously, 'I would be, and I know Gran would be too.' Hugh grinned sardonically at the omission, but Will pressed on regardless, 'And I expect Lucy would be really, because she's very anxious although she'd never say so, and she doesn't actually know what to do, any more than the rest of us.'

'And you think I do?' Hugh queried.

'Don't you?' Will countered simply.

'Alright, you scoot back, my lad, before you're missed. I'll get myself some breakfast and come round to see you officially. You can say I'm your legal adviser.' He smiled wryly but Will straightened his shoulders, as if a weight had been lifted off them.

'Okay, I'll tell Gran and Lucy. I don't expect she'll like it at first but she'll come round,' he said optimistically.

'I shouldn't count on it,' Hugh murmured as he showed Will out.

FOUR

Hugh returned to the kitchen, picked up his mug and stood with it in his hand, staring out of the window. Then he went back into the hall, up the stairs and into the bathroom. He put the mug down and showered quickly before dressing in dark trousers and a checked shirt. He was frowning, but when he abstractedly sipped at the cold coffee his expression changed to one of disgust. He went downstairs and made some more coffee, toasting a slice of bread at the same time.

He spent very little time over his abbreviated breakfast and, after checking his watch, left his breakfast things on the table. He was soon walking slowly down the track to the farmhouse, in and out of the faint beams of sunshine filtering through the oak trees. He was in luck, he realised with relief, seeing Philly Leygar walking towards him, holding a basket of milk cartons in one hand.

'Hello, Hugh,' she greeted him warmly. 'You're out early.'

'Yes, I wanted a quick word with you, Philly,' Hugh said bluntly. He felt a twinge of anxiety as the girl's open face clouded, and he found himself saying more than he had intended. 'Graham's been taken to hospital, and Jack doesn't seem to be around. I wondered if you knew where he is.'

Her eyes were concerned now. 'Oh dear, I'm so sorry. No, I don't know.' She looked down for a minute, and then back at

Hugh. 'He was rather unpleasant over dinner and, to be honest, he was drinking so much that I didn't want him to take me home, so I called Dad out to fetch me. Jack had driven off by the time he arrived, but I don't know where he was going, or even which way he went from The Mill.'

Hugh was frowning. 'Oh well, I expect he'll turn up when it suits him.' He turned and began walking back along the track with her. 'Did he talk much over dinner?' he asked, and saw her blush painfully. 'Other than about me and Anna,' he added cheerfully.

'Not really,' she said. 'It was mainly about himself,' she smiled suddenly, 'and how unfair life was being to him.'

'Oh,' Hugh was interested, 'did he say why?'

She shook her head. 'I wasn't really listening by then. I'm sorry.'

'Don't worry about it, Philly. I'm sure he'll turn up. I'm on my way to the manor so I'll take their milk with me, if you wouldn't mind dropping mine off.'

They stopped at the fork in the track and Philly took out one carton, handing the basket over to Hugh. 'It'll be easier if you take this,' she said. 'I can carry yours to the cottage. Do tell the family how sorry I am, and to let us know if we can do anything.' She turned in the direction of his cottage and he walked on towards the priory.

The warmth of the sun was already making itself felt, although a light breeze stroked his face. Above his head larks were singing their throbbing notes, soaring high over their territories on the rough turf meadow around the lake. On the track there was an occasional scuffling as rabbits scurried back into cover, white tails bobbing in alarm. A small weasel ran lithely across the rutted surface just in front of him, its body undulating smoothly, and Hugh noticed it automatically with the surface of his mind while his brain worked busily at this new problem.

He noticed the policeman standing inconspicuously inside

the priory gatehouse and walked over to him. 'A bad business,' he said. 'Who's in charge of the investigation?'

The young uniformed constable looked awkward, but replied, 'Inspector Elliot, sir.'

'Ah,' Hugh's expression lightened. 'Is that Inspector Robert Elliot who used to be with the Metropolitan Police?'

The policeman looked at him curiously and said, 'Yes, he's been with us for a couple of years.'

'Is he here now?' Hugh nodded at the priory buildings behind the constable.

'No, sir, but he'll be back shortly.'

'Fine, I expect I'll see him up at the house later.' He smiled at the look of alarm on the policeman's face. 'It's alright, constable. I know I can't go through the priory, I'll go round on the lower footpath.'

He raised his hand in farewell and set off on the path below the church, crossing the brook on the narrow plank bridge and coming out onto the back drive. Stopping for a moment, he looked down the drive towards the lodge but could not see any sign of Jack's distinctive BMW coupé, only a white police van. He turned towards the house again and his feet scrunched noisily on the newly weeded gravel as he strode along.

He crossed the courtyard between a police car and another van as Will appeared in the doorway of the house, Hades bursting out from behind his legs. 'Did you see the policeman in the gatehouse?' Will demanded, and Hugh nodded, fussing the dog and fending him away from the basket. Will carried on, 'There's another one by the bridge, d'you want to see?'

'Not right now, Will. I think I'd better come in for a bit before I see the sights.'

Will stood aside and Hugh passed him, pausing as he entered the cool dimness of the hall until his eyesight adjusted from the brightness outside. He held out the basket which Hades was sniffing hopefully. 'Here, I met Philly and collected your milk from her.'

'Oh, thanks.' Will took the basket and put it down on the floor by the sideboard. 'No,' he said sharply, 'leave it alone, Hades.' A sound in the corridor caught Hugh's attention and he turned to see Lucy standing by the door.

She came forward resolutely. 'I'm sorry Will tried to involve you in this, Hugh,' she said steadily. 'It's good of you to come, but I don't really see that there's anything you can do.'

He met her eyes, noting the signs of strain in her face, but before he could speak Isobel appeared behind her. 'Nonsense, my dear,' she said robustly, 'it was very clever of Will.' She said briskly to Hugh, 'Come through, we're in the sitting room.'

She turned and walked back along the corridor, and Hugh glanced amiably at Lucy, gesturing for her to go ahead of him. She stared at him crossly for a second, then made a moue of impatience and turned on her heel, stalking across the polished floorboards. Hugh smiled reassuringly at Will and preceded him to the sitting room, which the boy crossed to stand in front of the fireplace, taking Hades with him, one finger hooked in the big dog's collar.

Lucy was standing by the window, looking out unseeingly. The sunlight picked out red highlights in her chestnut hair and she looked very slight in her black jeans and dark green cotton shirt. Hugh studied her for a moment before turning to Isobel, who was sitting comfortably on an upright chair by the main table. Catching Hugh's eye she pointed to a worn armchair, where he seated himself without comment and waited. Juno came forward to greet him, her feathery tail waving slowly, before returning quietly to curl up by her mistress's feet.

Lucy turned abruptly to face them. 'This is nonsense,' she said, almost angrily. 'We're behaving as if there really is some-thing wrong, and I'm sure it's just police routine. There's really no need to drag Hugh into this.'

'No, dear,' her grandmother spoke firmly, 'we always need our friends when times are difficult, and I rather think this is going to be. It doesn't seem to me that this is purely routine for the police.' She looked at Hugh, her head cocked enquiringly.

'No,' he said evenly, returning her look searchingly. 'The police would automatically be called to the scene of an accident, but they certainly wouldn't take these precautions if they weren't harbouring suspicions of foul play.' The quiet words fell heavily into the silence of the room.

'But it has to be nonsense,' Lucy insisted, pushing her hair back with one hand. 'Who on earth would want to,' she hesitated fractionally, 'to hurt Graham?'

'Lucy, it isn't useful to baulk at the facts,' her grandmother said sternly, and Juno looked anxiously up into her face. 'Someone clearly has hurt him very badly, and we don't know that they didn't intend to kill him.' Lucy sat down suddenly on the window seat and let her curtain of hair fall forwards, partially hiding her face, but she did not say any more.

Hugh was watching Isobel. 'Has Jack appeared?' he asked.

She turned to him and replied, 'No, not yet. But,' she added, 'he doesn't seem to have left as his things are still at the lodge.' She smiled at his surprise. 'We have a key, and Lucy took it down to the policemen at the lodge. They took a quick look round and told her his clothes and laptop are still in his room.' She frowned, and ended, 'But nobody seems to have any idea where he is.'

Hugh thought briefly of the glowering man at the restaurant last night and decided not to mention Philly yet. He brought his thoughts back to the main issue. 'Do you have any idea why the police are so sure it couldn't be an accident? Will said there was a coping stone beside him, and Graham himself told me that several of them were loose.'

Isobel did not reply immediately, but stopped Will from speaking with a small gesture. 'Hush, dear, I think it may be better if we tell Hugh what we know one at a time.' Lucy looked up quickly, a surprised frown in her eyes, and opened her lips only to shut them again firmly. 'From the tenor of their questions it seemed to me that they thought the stone couldn't have fallen and hit him. So,' she continued hardily, 'presumably someone else must have picked it up and hit him with it.'

Hugh turned to Will, who was still standing on the rug in front of the fireplace, absently stroking Hades' curly head. 'Will, describe to me where you found him.'

Will came over eagerly and sat on the edge of the chair opposite Hugh, while Hades flung himself down heavily nearby. He leaned forwards, gesturing with his hands as he spoke. 'Well, you go over the bridge and there are a lot of bushes on the bank between the brook and the priory. You know how thick they are, but there's a bit of a path between them down to the lake.' Hugh nodded so Will carried on, swallowing awkwardly, and Hades put his head onto the boy's knee. 'His foot was sticking out behind a rhododendron just where the path curves left, so the rest of him was hidden by the bushes.'

'Was he lying on the path?' Hugh asked.

Will thought carefully before replying. 'No, more beside it, but a bit on it – his right arm was flung across it.'

'Did you think he'd been on the path when he fell?'

Will stared at him. 'Well, yes, I suppose I did. Why else would he have been there?'

'What did you think he was doing there?' Hugh persisted.

'We've been discussing that,' Isobel interjected, 'and we really don't have any idea. You see, Hugh, we thought at first that the accident had only just happened, and I suppose we imagined he'd remembered something he wanted to look at or to check. He's very conscientious.' She sighed. 'Better than we deserve, perhaps.'

Her hands twisted tightly together as she said, 'But then the doctor said that he must have been there for some time, probably since the early hours of the morning. We haven't been able to think what could have taken him there at such an odd time.'

Her eyes grew sorrowful. 'He must have lain there all those hours, and it's still so damp at night.'

'Could he have crawled there after he'd been hit, do you

think?' Lucy asked suddenly. 'Wouldn't that explain a lot?'

Hugh glanced understandingly at her. 'Yes, it would, of course. And it could be possible, depending on the severity of the wound, but ...'

'But,' Will interrupted, frowning, 'the stone was covered with blood and it was right beside him.'

'Yes, I thought that was what you'd said,' Hugh remarked. 'Where exactly was the stone when you found him?'

Will stared at him in surprise. 'Right by his head, of course. It was in the middle of the path, so you couldn't miss it.'

Hugh looked penetratingly at him and then turned to Isobel, who was watching him. 'That would be enough for the police,' he said.

'But what would be?' demanded Lucy, exasperated. 'If the stone was so obviously there, then he didn't try to crawl back but was still lying where it hit him.'

Isobel shook her head sharply and was about to speak, but Hugh forestalled her. 'You're not thinking, Lucy.' His tone was harsh. 'It's never pleasant to think of a possible assailant in the neighbourhood, perhaps among people we know, but you can't alter the facts.' His level gaze held her angry eyes. 'And don't you owe it to Graham to find the truth?'

She stared at him resentfully and then resolution gradually spread across her face. 'Yes, you're right. But why are you so sure that it was a deliberate attack?'

'Several points. If Graham had been on the path when he was hit he would have fallen more limply and partially onto the path, not stiffly sideways against the bushes.' He paused, waiting for her to comment, but she said nothing and he continued, 'The stone seems to be what struck him, so if he was on the path it couldn't have fallen from the wall – stones fall straight down, not at an angle.'

Lucy's eyes widened in understanding and she sat quite still, absorbing what he had said. 'So,' she said, thinking out the implications, 'someone must have picked up the stone, used it to hit him on the head and then dropped it when he fell.'

'Perhaps.' Hugh's voice was guarded, and she looked quickly across at him.

'You don't think so, do you?' Her brows drew together. 'What do you think happened?'

'I'm not sure yet.' He turned to Will, who was following the conversation closely. 'Did you see the police searching the ground?'

Will nodded. 'Yes, I watched them for a bit. They were looking through the bushes and on the path, and some of them looked about on the bridge and the track up to the church.'

'Did you notice whether they found anything?'

'I don't think they found anything big,' Will said thoughtfully, trying to remember just what he had seen. 'They mainly seemed to be picking things up from the ground and putting them in bags.'

'Anywhere in particular on the ground?'

Will frowned. 'Yes,' he said slowly. 'I thought at first they had found something in the bushes, but they really seemed more interested in the track near the prior's gateway.'

'Could you see what they were doing?' Hugh asked.

Will shook his head regretfully. 'No, I was too far away. But,' he was suddenly struck by a thought, 'they must have been picking up quite little things, because I did see some small bags being brought out.'

They all turned to Hugh, expecting him to speak, but he did not. He looked at them, saw that Isobel had already understood, and waited while Lucy and Will thought about it.

Lucy spoke first, having worked it out carefully. 'You mean that he was hit there and then hidden in the bushes?' She sounded disbelieving. 'But why on earth would somebody do that?'

'Perhaps he wasn't actually hidden,' Hugh said reflectively. 'It's possible that the police may have found traces to indicate that he was struck near the prior's gateway. Certainly that sort of stone would be readily to hand in the rubble there. No,' he spoke more definitely, 'I don't think he was hidden. Why should he be? If the attack took place in the early morning nobody was going to find him straight away; there was plenty of time for the assailant to get away.'

'They meant it to look like an accident!' Will burst out, almost shouting, and Hades leapt to his feet, startled. 'So they dragged him into the bushes and threw the stone down beside him.'

Lucy stared at Will and then looked across at Hugh, who said, 'Yes, I think it probably was like that. The assailant used the stone, so he didn't come with a weapon, just grabbed the nearest thing when he needed it. He was probably horrified at what he'd done and then tried to make it look like an accident, as Will's worked out.'

'But,' Lucy's voice dragged, 'Graham would know that it wasn't an accident. If he lives. So once they'd attacked him they must have meant to kill him.'

Hugh met her eyes and saw the horror in them. 'Not necessarily,' he said quietly. 'It would seem to be an unpremeditated attack. So the assailant probably hit out in alarm, maybe harder and perhaps more often than he needed to. And he may not have been thinking very clearly when he arranged the 'accident'; he certainly didn't arrange it very well.'

'But why?' Will asked abruptly. 'Lucy's right, you know. Why would anyone attack Graham? It just doesn't make sense.'

'Think it through,' Hugh advised. 'You'll see it for yourself.' He glanced across at Isobel again, and saw that she had followed his thoughts and had already reached the same conclusion.

Lucy was watching them both. 'You know why, don't you? And so do I.' Her voice was quite steady now. 'I can't think why Graham should have been out then, but I think he must have disturbed somebody who was doing something out there. And they weren't expecting Graham to be out at that time either, so they were caught by surprise. That's what you think happened, isn't it?'

They both agreed, and Will suddenly said, 'I bet I know what Graham was doing.' They all turned to look at him and he carried on rapidly, 'Just think of what's been happening. Mike had been here talking about the things we might be able to do with the old priory buildings, and we were all excited about it, even Graham, and making lots of plans. But I bet that when Graham went away he got worried about it. He didn't say anything about it yesterday, d'you remember? I bet that he got himself into a sweat about the buildings being damaged or spoiled, or something like that.'

'Yes, of course,' Lucy interrupted, 'he kept telling me that we mustn't go too fast, and should be cautious, but he always said that about everything so I didn't really notice anything strange. But you think he was so worried about it that he couldn't sleep, don't you, Will?' She looked enquiringly at her brother, who nodded. 'And then he came up here to look at the buildings and consider it. I think you're right; that's what he was doing,' she finished triumphantly, but then frowned. 'But what did he disturb? What is there here for anyone?'

She and Will looked expectantly at Hugh. Hades, scratching the hearthrug up around him, paused to look over too. 'No, that I can't answer,' Hugh said. 'We'll need more information before we can even begin to build a hypothesis.' He in turn looked enquiringly at Isobel, who smiled faintly.

'No, Hugh, I haven't the slightest idea what could be going on. But,' she said slowly, 'I do wonder why someone was doing whatever it was right now.'

Lucy and Will were clearly baffled, but Hugh regarded her with respect. 'You don't miss much,' he said quietly.

'But surely something could have been going on for a long time, couldn't it?' Lucy asked. 'None of us are likely to wander about the grounds in the early hours of the morning normally, so that when Graham did he also happened to come across whatever it was.'

'Yes, of course that's quite possible,' Isobel acknowledged, 'but I find it difficult to think what would attract an intruder back here time and again.' Lucy bit her lip and Isobel continued, 'It just seems to me that rather a lot of things have been happening just lately, and I can't help wondering if this intrusion is connected with them in some way.'

Will had followed this carefully. 'You mean the business about excavating the priory, and all that – Graham went out there because of it, and you think the intruder was there too for the same reason.'

His grandmother nodded. 'Yes, it may sound a little farfetched, but it does seem more than slightly coincidental.'

Will startled them all with a spurt of laughter. 'Oh Lord,' he said, spluttering with merriment, 'suppose Tilly was out prospecting for ghosts and mistook Graham for one and got into a panic.'

Hugh's lips twitched, but Isobel looked at Will reprovingly and Lucy spoke hastily, following her grandmother's line of thought. 'So you think the intruder doesn't like the thought of digging in the priory? But why on earth should he mind?'

'I know, the whole thing seems very puzzling,' Isobel admitted, 'but I think it is a possibility, however odd it may seem.'

'I agree, but,' Hugh entered a caveat, 'although I'm reluctant to destroy a plausible theory, Mike was only down here a couple of days ago. How many people could already know about the ideas and plans you discussed with him?'

Lucy smiled. 'The whole village I should think, if not most of the valley by now.' Her smile widened when she saw Hugh's expression of disbelief. 'Anna and Simon were here when Mike came, there's no reason why either of them shouldn't have talked about them. And Mike was a stranger here so a lot of people would have noticed him and asked questions about him, who he was and what he was doing. I shouldn't be at all surprised if they made up the answers too.'

Isobel looked at Hugh's startled face. 'Oh yes, it's very quiet

here, so people are always interested in something even slightly
out of the ordinary. You were a source of great interest yourself
when you first arrived, you know.' They were all amused at the
look of horror that crossed Hugh's face.

'It's alright,' Lucy mocked gently, 'you've been superseded
now.'

Before Hugh had time to answer Will spoke again in a
discouraged tone. 'But that means it could have been almost
anyone. Or more than one person.'

'If we accept the theory,' Hugh agreed. 'But don't forget that
there may be other reasons behind the attack too.' He looked
round at them. 'In the meantime I think it would be best if you
don't talk to anybody else, other than the police, about what
happened or what we've discussed.'

'Why not?' Lucy sounded indignant. 'We've talked to you
about it.'

Hugh smiled at her affably. 'But then I've been retained by
the head of the family as his legal adviser.'

'What!' Lucy was becoming angry. 'Don't be silly, Hugh. We
don't need one, and even if we did you aren't one anyway.'

Isobel intervened. 'Will is quite right, Lucy, and has unwittingly chosen very well.' Her grandson looked at her, startled, as
she turned to Hugh and held out her hand. 'We're very grateful,
Hugh, and we will do as you advise. All of us,' she stressed,
looking pointedly at her irritated granddaughter.

Hugh took her hand and gazed thoughtfully at her upright
figure. 'You know, don't you? How?'

Isobel smiled faintly. 'I was staying in London with a friend
of the Benton family when the case was on. She was naturally
concerned and followed the proceedings closely. The pictures in
the newspapers were a very good likeness.'

'Gran, what on earth do you mean?' Will was confused and
turned to Hugh. 'I didn't think you really meant it, about being
our legal adviser, you know.'

'And yet he's a very good one, Will,' his grandmother said.

'He's a very well-known barrister, or solicitor,' she smiled apologetically at Hugh, 'I can never remember which is which. And he'll know exactly what we should do, so we'll do as he says.' She looked across the room at Lucy, who met her gaze and nodded reluctantly. 'And now,' Isobel suggested, 'why don't we have some coffee. I'm sure we could all do with some.'

'I'll make it.' Lucy got up and went out of the room, and Isobel turned to Hugh. 'Do you think ...' she began, to be interrupted by a thunderous knocking on the courtyard door. She looked round, startled, as Hades sprang up, barking loudly, and shot out of the room.

Jack's loud hectoring tones came nearer and Will went quickly to the door. 'Get this damned dog away,' Jack snapped at him and Will put a hand through Hades' collar, pulling him back as he snarled and struggled.

'What the hell is going on?' Jack asked, pushing past Will into the sitting room and leaving Lucy standing in the doorway. 'There's a copper at the lodge refusing to let me in and jabbering about an accident.'

Hugh eyed him pensively. He was wearing the clothes he had worn last night, slightly dishevelled now, and clearly had not shaved yet, his dark stubble contrasting badly with the pallor of his face, while a strong smell of stale alcohol emanated from him.

'I'm afraid Graham has been hurt,' Isobel said carefully. 'He was found near the priory a short time ago and should be in the hospital by now.'

'What happened to him?' Jack demanded, shocked.

'He had a nasty blow to the head,' Isobel replied, trying to quieten the little spaniel who stood defensively in front of her, yapping furiously. 'It looks as though one of the coping stones fell and struck him.'

'What the hell was the old fool doing up there at night?' Jack demanded rudely, and Hades' low rumbling growl grew louder.

Isobel's brows drew together and she spoke more coldly.

'We don't know yet, but ...'

He interrupted her, saying forcefully, 'And it sounds as though you'll be liable for his injuries. That's likely to cost you a few thousand.'

Isobel stared at him with distaste, but it was Hugh who spoke next. 'The police were looking for you,' he said deliberately, watching Jack's face, which tightened. 'We should let them know you're here.'

'What the hell for?' Jack demanded. 'It's got nothing to do with me.'

'You are his nephew,' Hugh pointed out gently, 'and may be able to explain why he was at the priory, especially as you seem to know he was there during the night.'

'Mr bloody Clever, aren't you?' Jack jeered nastily. 'The copper at the house told me. And,' he ground out angrily, 'I wasn't here, so how should I know what he was doing?'

'Mmm, they did wonder where you were,' Hugh said quietly.

'Bloody police, always poking their noses in,' Jack muttered crossly, and then met Hugh's eyes defiantly. 'I went clubbing in Corrington, and yes,' he added with a malicious smile, 'I had good company too, not that little farm girl who has to be at home before the cock crows. You're not the only one who can pull the beauties. I bet you had a good evening yourself,' he sneered.

Lucy's gaze sharpened, and Isobel intervened. 'I wonder if we could ring up the hospital to find out how Graham is, or is it too soon?'

'I should ring them,' Hugh advised. 'If they can't tell you anything yet, they may be able to let you know when they can.'

She nodded and moved over to the small table near the window where the handset rested, closely followed by the little spaniel.

'I should be doing that,' Jack said sharply. 'After all, I'm related to him.'

Isobel ignored him and picked up the telephone, just as there was a knock on the courtyard door. Pausing, she glanced round. 'Will, would you answer that? Take them into the drawing room, and please take Hades with you. I don't expect I shall be long. Lucy,' she glanced at her granddaughter, 'that coffee would be very welcome.'

Hugh stood up as Will and Lucy left the room, taking a glowering Hades with them, but Isobel waved a hand to stop him from leaving. He picked up the newspaper and began to glance through it as she dialled, while Jack fidgeted with the ornaments on the mantelpiece. Hugh's attention was caught suddenly by the voices in the hall, but Isobel spoke briefly into the telephone, waited for a time, and then spoke again, listening intently to the reply. She too had heard the voices in the hall while she was waiting, and a slight frown creased her forehead for a moment.

When she put the handset down she turned soberly to the men. 'They're waiting for the results of x-rays, but he hasn't recovered consciousness. All they'll say is that he's critically ill; they won't give a prognosis.' She sighed. 'Graham didn't deserve this. He's such a good man and he's done well for our family. Better than Will and Lucy can perhaps appreciate yet.' Jack snorted, but she turned towards the door. 'That sounded like Tilly and Simon. We'd better bring them in here.'

She walked along the corridor and across the hall to the drawing room, returning immediately with Will and the visitors, Hades close behind them and watching their movements vigilantly. Tilly entered the room first and noticed Hugh at once. 'Hugh!' she exclaimed. 'So you've heard too. How on earth did you find out so quickly? The postman told me and of course I had to come straight up here.'

Hugh noticed with distaste how avidly her eyes were gleaming, but was spared the need to answer as Tilly swung round without a pause. 'Jack, how awful for you. I just couldn't believe it was true, but Will has been telling us about it. They're saying the most awful things in the village, of course.' She spoke with relish but had to stop to draw breath, and Simon immediately took his opportunity.

'We met on the drive,' he explained and continued tentatively, 'I heard a rather fantastic story in the shop and wondered what could be behind it.' He turned to Hugh. 'You obviously heard something too?'

Hugh nodded blandly but did not speak, and Isobel said pleasantly, 'My dears, it is so kind of you to come.' Will looked across at Hugh and met his eyes for a pregnant moment, but his grandmother continued, 'I'm afraid we're a bit disorganised, but I'm sure Will has explained to you what's happened. Do sit down.' She turned to her grandson. 'Will, please let Lucy know that Tilly and Simon have called so that she can bring some extra cups.'

Will left the room without a word, and Simon spoke hastily, 'Mrs Rossington, I haven't come to intrude, just to say how sorry I am about Graham and to see if there's anything I can do.' He turned to the man hulking near her and glaring angrily at him. 'Of course, Jack, you must say if there's anything I can do to help you too.'

Tilly was nodding fervently in agreement as he spoke and burst out, 'Yes, indeed, that's just why I've come. It must be so awful for you. In fact, I couldn't believe that it was true when I heard it. You really can't believe everything you hear,' she ended meaningfully.

'I gather from Will that Graham really has been injured,' Simon said quickly. 'How is he?'

'I wish we knew,' Isobel replied. 'The nurse at the hospital was very reticent.'

'But what on earth happened?' Simon demanded, and then apologised. 'I'm sorry, I don't mean to be nosey, but there's some ridiculous story going the rounds that he was attacked, and that seems too far-fetched to be true.'

'What!' Jack exploded. 'You've kept that pretty quiet.' He

glared round at the Rossingtons, his head thrusting forward belligerently on his thick shoulders.

'I don't know the truth of the matter myself,' Isobel admitted candidly, watched greedily by Tilly from a chair by the fireplace. 'Will found Graham unconscious in the bushes near the prior's gateway this morning, and when the doctor came he didn't seem to be satisfied with the circumstances, so he called in the police.' She spread her hands. 'We can hardly believe it ourselves, but the village tale seems to be accurate for once.' She smiled wryly, and then caught Simon's expression of consternation. 'What else have you heard? There is something, isn't there?'

He hesitated, and Tilly leaned forward, saying eagerly, 'Oh, it's a lot of nonsense, of course, you know how people talk. Nobody would believe that sort of story. After all, anybody who knows her really couldn't think for a minute that Lucy would bang Graham on the head to get him out of the way, so that her plans for the priory could go ahead. Could they?' she asked disingenuously.

Simon began angrily, 'Of course they couldn't ...' before he was interrupted.

'So that's it,' Jack said aggressively, and Hades sprang up again from the hearth rug, his hackles rising. 'I know the poor old beggar was worried about it. He gave his life to this place, but now he's beginning to get in the way of your plans for making more money.' They were shocked at the malevolence in his face. 'Well, I'll see that you don't get away with this.'

Hugh cut in, his voice hard and level. 'You'd better watch what you say, Jack. If,' he stressed the word, 'if it was a deliberate attack the police will regard us all as suspects.'

Jack glared at him. 'I'll have plenty to tell the police,' he said loudly, 'and this is one case you won't get to stitch up.' Then he turned and stormed out of the room, barging past Lucy who was standing in the doorway holding the coffee tray.

There was a stunned silence. Only Tilly moved, turning to gaze curiously at Hugh, who was looking after Jack, one eyebrow raised in surprise. She said longingly, 'Perhaps I should go after him,' but sat back in her chair when Simon, glancing apologetically at Lucy, turned to Isobel.

He said quietly, 'You'd better know, I suppose. There's some tale of a row between Graham and Lucy over the priory, and of course that's developing as it's repeated.'

'Into the fabrication that Tilly has so kindly repeated?' Isobel asked evenly, as Hades subsided into silent watchfulness.

'Well,' Simon spoke reluctantly, 'yes, something of the sort. I overheard two old dears in the shop discussing something similar.'

'It livens up their rather dull lives,' Lucy said calmly. She came into the room with the tray, followed by Will, who glowered angrily at Tilly and Simon. 'Jack obviously likes the idea, but nobody else is going to take that sort of story seriously as long as we don't fuss about it.'

'No, of course they're not going to,' Simon said quickly, and Tilly rushed into speech, cutting him off. 'I just thought it was better for you to know what's being said. You know how people will always say there's no smoke without fire.'

Will stared at her contemptuously, but Lucy replied quite calmly, 'Thank you, Tilly, it was very thoughtful of you.' Her brother had a sudden fit of coughing and she waited until the paroxysm had subsided. 'Do sit down, Simon, and don't worry about it. All sorts of people won't be able to resist hinting at the story or just telling me obliquely for my own good, so we'd have heard it soon enough.'

'That's just what I thought,' Tilly agreed mendaciously, sitting down too. 'It's at times like this that you find out who your friends are.'

Will pointedly ignored her and spoke trenchantly to the room in general. 'No one would believe such nonsense anyway.'

Lucy smiled at him affectionately as she resumed her seat in the window, holding her coffee cup carefully. 'Gran, did you ring the hospital?'

Her grandmother nodded, and Lucy continued, 'Can they say how he is?'

Isobel shook her head. 'They couldn't tell me much just yet. I have to ring back later.'

'Has he come round at all?' Will asked quickly.

'No,' Isobel replied, 'I'm afraid he hasn't.'

'But he will, won't he?' Simon asked her. 'Have they any idea how serious his injuries are?'

'Bad, from the sounds of it,' Hugh answered. 'Whoever attacked him was pretty thorough.'

Isobel handed Will the plate of biscuits and he picked one up automatically, putting it into the mouth he had opened in astonishment at Hugh's frankness.

Simon did not notice this byplay, his forehead creased in a worried frown, but before he could speak again Tilly said with relish, 'Just think, it could be somebody we know.' She looked at their surprised faces and explained, 'The person who attacked Graham, of course. Quite mad I expect. I believe you quite often don't see any signs of madness in people who seem perfectly ordinary until something like this happens.'

Will could not help himself. 'But then again some people are quite obviously mad anyway.'

Even Isobel's lips twitched when Tilly agreed earnestly, 'Yes, I know, but I don't think there's anyone like that around here.'

'But in a sense Tilly is right,' Simon said, still frowning. 'Why should anyone in their senses attack Graham?'

'We haven't the faintest idea,' Lucy replied from the window seat, 'but we may know more when the police return.'

'Are you expecting them again?' Tilly asked, obviously thrilled at the prospect.

'Yes,' Lucy said. 'The police sergeant came in before he left and said they'd be back later today.'

'And they've left two policemen here,' Will said with intent.

'Ooh, in the house?' Tilly squealed, looking round as if she had overlooked a uniformed figure in a corner of the room.

'No,' Will responded scornfully. 'By the priory buildings.' He glanced at Simon. 'Didn't you see one at the lodge too?'

Simon shook his head. 'I came up the farm drive from the village as soon as I heard the rumours in the shop. I called in to see if Hugh had heard anything, and when he wasn't there I came on up here. Why have they left them there?'

'They're guarding the site of the crime,' said Will with relish.

Hugh intervened. 'They won't want the ground disturbed before they can examine it in detail, especially by people like Will trampling all over it looking for clues.' He ignored Will's protests and added, 'It's fortunate that the weather's holding up.'

Simon was looking at him, puzzled. 'The ground? How will that help them?'

'There are all sorts of traces they might find,' Hugh replied noncommittally, and Simon stared at him, before saying, 'You seem to know a lot about it.'

'A fair amount,' Hugh said. Isobel caught her grandson's eye as he was about to join the conversation and he subsided unwillingly.

'Isn't it exciting?' Tilly burst out excitedly. 'Oh of course, I know it's awful about poor Graham,' she said perfunctorily, 'but it's so exciting to be on the scene of the crime, as it were, and even perhaps to know the attacker.' Her gaze drifted inadvertently towards Lucy, but before anyone could speak there was another knock on the courtyard door which made them all start.

'I expect that's the police this time,' Lucy said, rising to her feet. 'I'll let them in.' She smiled at Simon, who got up as she passed his chair, saying, 'I'd better get out of the way, but do let me know if I can do anything.'

She nodded and thanked him quietly before she left the room. Simon turned to Tilly and held out a hand. 'Come on, Tilly, walk back with me.' She rose reluctantly to her feet, and Simon glanced at Hugh, who still sat at ease in his armchair.

'I've got those mugs you wanted. I fired them last night. Do you want to come down and choose your own?'

Hugh nodded, but stayed where he was. 'Yes, I'd like to do that. I'll drop by later on.'

Simon gazed at him indecisively, but the sound of footsteps in the corridor made him turn hastily and hurry towards the door, followed more slowly by Tilly. He came to a sudden stop when Lucy ushered two men into the room, and a smile twitched involuntarily at his lips as he stared at them.

The older of the two men was just over six feet tall and slim, with curly brown hair and a tanned skin, while the younger was of middle height and middle girth, so that he looked rather square. The elder had cool grey eyes which looked at Simon with interest, while the younger sergeant was assessing him expertly from the shrewd blue eyes that twinkled in his rubicund face.

Lucy introduced them, as the two dogs came cautiously up to sniff the newcomers, relaxing when they recognised the trousers from an earlier visit that morning. 'Detective Inspector Elliot and Detective Sergeant Peters. This is Tilly Barlow and Simon Trent, friends from the village. They're just leaving.'

Tilly stared avidly at the two men, one finger abstractedly twisting a wispy curl, while the introductions were acknowledged. Simon muttered a few words and she smiled ingratiatingly at them, before reluctantly following him as he slid gratefully through the doorway.

Lucy took them to the courtyard door and returned immediately to find that her grandmother had just turned to Hugh. 'This is Hugh Carey,' she began, and the inspector nodded. 'We've met before,' he said.

'We have indeed. How are you, Elliot?' Hugh was on his feet, holding out his hand with a friendly smile.

'Well, and busy,' the inspector responded, shaking his hand, 'and rather surprised to find you involved here.' He ended his comment with a note of enquiry.

'It's quite simple, really,' Hugh replied. 'I'm staying in an estate cottage to do some freelance work, and I've been retained professionally by the head of the family to represent their interests.'

Will blushed as the inspector glanced at him, before returning his gaze to Hugh. 'Is that so?' he asked gravely. 'And what is your own connection with the victim?'

'Oh I've met him, so you'll need a statement from me,' Hugh acknowledged. 'Do you know that Graham's nephew has turned up? In fact, he's just left here.'

'Yes, we found him in the courtyard, about to get into a very flashy sports car. I advised him against driving it anywhere,' he added evenly. 'He seems very keen to speak to us, so he's waiting with one of my men.'

'I'm sure he is,' Hugh said levelly. 'He's rather keen to keep any pointing fingers away from him.' He looked at the policeman. 'Can you let us know how things stand?'

'Yes, to some extent I can do that,' the inspector said, taking the seat by the fireplace that Tilly had vacated, which gave him a clear view of everybody in the room. Hades lay nearby on the rug, surveying the scene just as carefully. The sergeant sat discreetly on an upright chair near the door, out of everyone's immediate line of sight, and took out a fat notebook.

'We've been over the ground thoroughly and have established a fairly comprehensive scenario,' the inspector began. Will leaned forward, drinking in his words, and in the background Sergeant Peters had to smother a grin. 'Mr Rother had crossed the bridge over the brook,' it took the Rossingtons aback to hear Graham called by his surname, but they recovered quickly and listened intently to the unfolding narrative, 'and walked as far as the first gateway ...'

'The prior's gateway,' Will interjected, and the inspector nodded and continued. 'As far as the prior's gateway when he was attacked. His assailant seems to have grabbed a heavy stone from the pile of rubble against the wall,' his auditors nodded knowledgeably at this point, 'and struck him heavily on the back of the head. Mr Rother fell on the spot and at least two more blows were struck when he lay on the ground. We found traces of blood on the flagstones inside the gateway and, although we are still awaiting the results of tests, they're almost certain to be Mr Rother's.'

The inspector paused, looking round the room shrewdly, studying the faces that watched him. 'None of you seem to be surprised by this,' he said at last, looking towards Isobel.

She smiled wryly. 'Inspector, we've thought and talked of nothing else since you left, and came to this conclusion shortly before you appeared.'

'Oh,' he was interested, 'on what grounds?'

Hugh answered, 'Nothing that's likely to be of use to you, I'm afraid, Elliot. Our deductions were mainly based on observations of where your men had been searching.' Sergeant Peters glanced quickly at Will and saw the boy's face was tinged with red again. 'And,' Hugh continued, 'Will's description of Graham's position when he found him.'

The inspector said to the room at large, 'Very acute of you.' He smiled at them and then continued with his account. 'The assailant dragged Mr Rother along the side of the track, where we've found more slight traces of blood, and placed him on the path through the shrubbery, partially concealed by the bushes. He then went back for the stone that he had used in the attack and left it neatly beside his victim's head.'

He felt Hugh's eyes watching him intently and glanced towards him, meeting his gaze blandly, before looking round at the other three people listening to him. 'It looks like an attempt to disguise the attack as an accident. It was a poor attempt,' he said judicially. 'The attack happened between one and three o'clock this morning, according to the preliminary medical report. I shall need statements from all of you as to your whereabouts at that time,' his lips twisted, 'and I want to know anything further you may have observed or may know about the matter.'

He looked across at Isobel. 'Is there a room you can let me use without too much disruption to the household?'

Her face expressed the distress she had experienced as the inspector described the attack on Graham, and Juno pressed comfortingly against her legs, but she said immediately, 'Yes, of course. We'll help in any way we can. I think the study is likely to be the most suitable room for your purposes.' She glanced at Lucy, who nodded in agreement. 'It's on the far side of the house, near the internal door to the estate office.' She looked at the inspector enquiringly, 'Would you like me to show you now?'

'Yes, please, that sounds just right.' He rose to his feet, followed by the sergeant, and held open the door for Isobel.

As soon as the policemen had gone, Will turned to Hugh. 'You know him,' he said bluntly to Hugh.

'Yes,' Hugh acknowledged. 'He was involved in a case I worked on. I didn't realise he'd moved out of London.'

'What was the case?' Will asked eagerly.

'Nothing like this,' Hugh replied. 'A straightforward one of fraud and intimidation.'

'Oh,' said Will, clearly disappointed.

'It can't have been at all pleasant,' Lucy commented, watching Hugh's face, 'but then I don't suppose any of your cases were.'

'No,' he answered, 'but that's inevitable, and mainly behind me now.'

FIVE

The inspector stood in the doorway of the study. Like the sitting room, it had a mullioned window looking out on the overgrown front drive, and French windows opening onto a narrow side terrace. Beyond this a small lawn led down to the track that connected the front and back drives. The room was similar in size to the sitting room, but looked smaller as all of the cream-coloured walls were lined with shelves that were full to overflowing with books, books that were stacked haphazardly, and sometimes a little precariously, in heaps. The inspector looked round appraisingly, noting the practical desk at an angle between the windows, and the mixture of deep armchairs and rigid upright chairs. He turned to Isobel, who waited just inside the room, and said, 'This will do very well. I'd like to start with your statement.'

'Yes, of course. I shall be very glad to tell you anything I can,' she responded.

Indicating a chair to the sergeant, who placed himself on it at the side of the room near the door, Inspector Elliot brought an upright chair forward and placed it at the front of the desk for Isobel. She seated herself, her profile outlined against the deep red curtains, with the sunlight coming through the window falling on her face.

The inspector went round the desk, pulled out the leather

wing chair and sat down opposite her. 'Now, Mrs Rossington, can we start with what you were doing between one and three o'clock this morning?'

'Sleeping in my room, I'm afraid,' she replied.

He accepted the inevitability of this. 'Did you hear anything, however slight?'

She shook her head reluctantly. 'No, I'm afraid I didn't. I slept quite soundly, and as I'm generally rather a light sleeper I'm usually easily disturbed.'

He nodded, and the sergeant scribbled quietly in his notebook. 'Which room is yours?' the inspector asked.

'The west room, at the far end of the house from the priory,' she answered. 'It overlooks the front and has a window looking west, too.'

'Thank you. Now, can you give me some idea of how long you've known Mr Rother?'

'Certainly,' she said. 'I've known him all his life, or at least since he was a very small boy. His father,' she explained, 'came here as my husband's estate manager. He was a widower, with a son and daughter. Angela was the elder and wasn't really very happy here, but Graham loved it. He was much of an age with my own son, Francis, so they grew up together and were very close, although somewhat dissimilar in outlook. I believe that Graham always felt that Francis didn't care enough about the estate, while to Graham it meant a great deal. But it was Francis's inheritance and he felt more strongly about it than he perhaps showed, taking it for granted in a way that Graham couldn't understand.'

Her hands moved from her lap to the armrests of the chair, and she continued, 'Anyway, after my daughter-in-law died my son began to travel and was away for long spells. When the senior Mr Rother died, Graham was the obvious choice to succeed his father as the estate manager. He has always been very good at the job, and has found ways of keeping the estate together against rather heavy odds. Without him we would certainly have had to sell parts of it quite some time ago.' She looked reflective. 'I don't know if you will understand what I mean, but I have sometimes felt that he cares too much for it. He loves every stick and stone of the place and is inclined to fight to keep it as it is, staving off alterations and changes with all his might.'

She added quickly, 'Don't misunderstand me, we more than appreciate what he does, but I think perhaps that he should have something more to care about in his life. For the Rossingtons, you see, the manor is just here, as it always has been, and they will fight for it if it should be threatened, but otherwise they just take it for granted as they go about their lives, with other loves and interests.'

The inspector met her eyes. 'Yes, I think I do understand. People do react that way sometimes. What family does Mr Rother have?'

'We've always thought of him as part of ours,' she responded quietly. 'Not by blood, perhaps, but always by affection and long ties of custom. His father has been dead for many years, and Graham and Angela were never close. She lives in London, and married a dealer in antiques, I think. Jack is her son.'

'Is he a frequent visitor?' the inspector asked.

'No, as far as I know he hasn't been down here since a single visit when he was about twelve. But,' she offered, 'I think he probably has his mother's urban inclinations'

Inspector Elliot shifted in his chair. 'Do you know why he's visiting now?'

'He said,' Isobel emphasised the word slightly, 'that he was touring in the area, apparently.'

'Ah. Has he moved on?'

'I don't really know. Neither he nor Graham mentioned his plans, but I gather his belongings are still in the lodge,' Isobel replied evenly.

'I see. Did Mr Rother never marry?' the inspector continued.

'No,' she spoke regretfully. 'I used to wish he would, until I realised no woman could ever compete with his,' she hesitated, searching for a word, 'his obsessive love for the estate. I don't believe he ever willingly spends time away from it.'

'Do you know of anyone who might bear him a grudge?' the inspector asked.

'No. I've thought and thought about it since it became obvious that his injuries weren't caused by accident, but I really can't imagine that anyone would want to hurt him.' She met the inspector's gaze steadily. 'He's a kindly man who wouldn't knowingly hurt a soul. All he ever does is bore or irritate people with his stories and his attitude to the priory. That wouldn't be enough to provoke an attack.'

'No, I think however profound the boredom or irritation, it would be unlikely to lead to this form of revenge.' The inspector smiled. 'Well, can you think of any reason why he might have been in the grounds so early in the morning?'

'We've talked about that, of course, and I believe Will and Lucy between them may have hit on the answer.' His enquiring look encouraged her to go on. 'There has been some excitement about the old priory buildings in the last few days – some new and perhaps startling prospects and ideas that we've been discussing, rather interminably.' A rueful expression crossed her face as she spoke.

'Will and Lucy think that Graham may have become concerned about this and perhaps been unable to sleep, so that he got up and walked over to the old priory, trying to sort out his thoughts. I must say I think it's very likely that something of the sort may have been behind his presence there at that odd hour.' She added reflectively, 'Though what he might have found we can't imagine. There isn't anything there that anyone could want that badly.'

'What have your priory discussions been about?' Inspector Elliot enquired.

'Well, Hugh was interested after Graham showed him around the buildings, and he spoke to an archaeologist friend of his, who paid us a flying visit.' She suddenly smiled warmly. 'Mike Shannon. A very energetic young man, very pleasant indeed.' She turned to the sergeant, who was still scribbling busily in his notebook. 'I don't know his address I'm afraid, but of course Hugh will.' She turned back to the inspector. 'Anyway, Mike was very excited about the place and talked about excavations and renovations and conversions, and all manner of things that might be possible one day.'

Her manner became deprecating. 'His enthusiasm was very contagious and we all got excited, even, I think, Graham. But, discussing it just now, we've realised that although we continued talking about possibilities among ourselves, Graham tended to avoid the subject or try to play it down.'

'What is so exciting about the old priory?' the inspector asked curiously.

Isobel looked at him in amusement. 'I know. Strange, isn't it? But apparently the fact that the buildings have remained virtually untouched opens up all sorts of historical and archaeological possibilities. Don't ask me what,' she added hastily, 'you'd better get Mike to explain those to you. He'll do it very well.'

'I'm sure he will,' the inspector said unenthusiastically, and the sergeant hid a grin behind one large hand.

'Anyway,' Isobel went on, 'Mike says that people like to visit and stay in places like the old priory, so that's something we're going to consider in the long term.'

'Yes, I believe many people do like that sort of place,' agreed Inspector Elliot, who found this incomprehensible himself. 'So, do you feel Mr Rother isn't happy with these ideas?'

'Well, he hasn't said anything yet, but he very probably has had second, and third, thoughts about them. Still, they're only ideas at the moment, and will need a lot of consideration before much can come of them. Graham can nearly always be brought round in the end.'

'I see,' he said. 'Have you any idea what an intruder might

have been doing in the grounds, that would necessitate such a violent attack to prevent discovery?'

'No, none at all. A lot of the locals use the paths and tracks in the grounds, of course. The ones from the village to the farm and the church are the most popular, but people using them wouldn't need to come through the buildings, or to the prior's gateway. Anyway,' she added meditatively, 'I can't see what any of the locals would be doing out at that time of the morning. Oh,' she recalled, 'of course, there's Simon Trent who's doing some metal detecting in the grounds, but again I shouldn't imagine that he'd want to be doing it at that time. And even if he did, Graham knows all about it.'

'Does he approve of it?' the inspector asked in surprise.

'Oh no, not at all,' Isobel said equably. 'But he's coming round to it.'

'Did you give Mr Trent permission yourself?' the inspector queried.

'No, Lucy did, but I didn't object. What harm can he do? And in fact he's found some of the lead labels from the Victorian plantings, which will help us to restore the grounds one day. That was bringing Graham round. Oh, and the old fish trap that Simon discovered near the lake helped.'

'I see,' the inspector commented dryly. He considered Isobel for a moment and then asked, 'Have you started doing any work on the priory buildings already?'

'No, not yet. Mike was insistent that everything should be left untouched.' She smiled faintly, and the inspector spoke again.

'Can you think of anybody who might have cause to damage the priory buildings?'

She stared at him in astonishment. 'Who on earth would want to do something like that?' Her voice sharpened. 'Have they been damaged?'

'Yes, it looks as though they have. Nothing very much,' he added quickly, 'but I should like you all to come down there with me later and give me your opinions.'

'Very well,' Isobel said, frowning, and he stood up, saying, 'Well, I think that's all for now. Sergeant Peters will get this typed up, and I will ask you to check and sign it when it's done. But if you should remember anything else, anything at all, please do let us know at once. Even something that seems quite insignificant may be very important.'

'Of course I will,' she responded, rising to her feet. 'We won't be thinking of much else, I imagine.'

'Would you ask your granddaughter to come in next, please, and then wait for us in the hall.' She nodded, and thanked the sergeant as he opened the door for her. 'Oh, Mrs Rossington,' the inspector spoke just as she was leaving, 'it will be useful if I can get some idea of the layout of the house. Could somebody show me over it later on?'

'Yes, of course. Just let us know when you're ready,' she replied, wondering why.

Lucy knocked on the door of the study and the sergeant opened it, ushering her into the room. The inspector came round the desk and held the chair for her. 'Take a seat, Miss Rossington.' She sat down with a word of thanks and looked expectantly across the desk at him as he resumed his place.

'Miss Rossington,' he said, 'your grandmother has explained that she has always believed Mr Rother to be virtually a member of the family. Do you feel that yourself?'

Lucy was not expecting this question, and sat back, considering it. 'Well, yes, I suppose I do,' she said slowly, a note of surprise in her voice. She looked across at Inspector Elliot, who was watching her. 'I've never really thought about it before. We've regarded him as a bit of a pain at times, with his harping on about the priory,' she made a small moue, 'but he's always been here, more than our father was really. We've always relied on him, without perhaps realising it until now, even down to taking our toys to him to be mended when we were little.' She sat up straighter. 'Yes, Graham's as much family as anyone can be.'

'Your grandmother has explained the theory you and your brother have about Mr Rother's presence in the grounds in the early hours of the morning,' he said. 'How did you arrive at it?'

'It really is only a theory,' Lucy said quickly, 'but it does fit in with what has been happening, and with Graham's attitude.'

'What has been happening?' he persisted.

'Well,' she paused to collect her thoughts, 'it's a bit complicated. You see, when our father died we found that it was going to be rather hard to keep the house and the estate, but we decided we'd try to.' She met his eyes defiantly. 'A lot of people think we're mad, but it's ours and we care about it.' A little pinkness had stolen into her cheeks. 'Anyway,' a gamine smile lit her face, 'at least Graham agreed with us about that.'

'Was it unusual for him to agree with you?' he asked gravely.

She nodded emphatically. 'Oh yes. We generally don't have the same views at all, but I suppose it wasn't really noticeable until Daddy died.'

'Why was that?'

'Well,' she explained, 'I didn't have anything to do with the running of the estate while Daddy was alive, and anyhow I've been away at university for the last four years, so there was nothing for Graham and me to clash over.'

'But you have clashed with him recently?'

'Oh yes, frequently,' she said frankly. 'Basically, we agree about keeping the estate going for Will. He's sixteen now,' she added, 'so that's really for the next five or six years. But,' she pushed a strand of chestnut hair behind her ear, and went on, 'we didn't really agree about how to do it.'

'What does Mr Rother want to do?' the inspector asked her, feeling sure he knew already.

'That's just it.' She took a deep breath. 'He doesn't want

to do anything, just carry on as things are. He says we should retrench and save money, but he doesn't want to do anything positive that might bring in more cash.' She looked exasperated. 'He particularly doesn't want to do anything that might affect the old priory buildings.'

'And you do?' he queried gently.

'Well, not particularly, or at least not until recently. We're planning to offer cream teas in the tourist season – you know, tables on the lawn in fine weather and sitting indoors in the hall otherwise. We were hoping to start at Easter, but I don't know whether we can now,' she finished bleakly.

'Mr Rother doesn't approve of this scheme?'

'No, not at all, but we really do have to earn some money, not just make savings.' Lucy spoke emphatically.

'Why does he disapprove of it?' Inspector Elliot asked curiously.

Lucy shrugged. 'I don't really know. It was something new, and he always takes time to come round to new things and new people. I expect he was worried that the visitors might wander over to the priory and scrawl graffiti on the walls, or take bits of stone as souvenirs.'

'I understand you do now have plans to encourage visitors to come to the old priory?' he asked.

'No, there aren't any plans as such, but we've just been made to realise that the priory buildings could be an asset. It's still a new idea to us, and although it sounds wildly exciting we haven't done more than discuss various possibilities. Endlessly.' She smiled ruefully and added, 'That's what Will and I think was behind Graham's presence in the grounds in the early morning. We think he was worrying about all this, and because he couldn't sleep he went walking through the buildings to think things out.'

'I see,' the inspector commented. 'Who would have the final say about these proposals?'

Lucy looked blank. 'Well, I suppose we would have just

thrashed them out until we'd reached some sort of consensus. Graham wouldn't veto anything outright if we all wanted it, he just wouldn't actually agree to it. But,' she added slowly, 'I suppose Gran and I would make the final decision if it came to that.'

She looked across at the inspector. 'You see, we're all trustees for Will, but Graham looks after the estate's finances while Gran and I look after the family interests.' She paused for a moment. 'I don't know if it actually says it like that in the Trust document, but that's how we've always interpreted it.'

'Has Mr Rother too?' he asked neutrally.

'Oh yes, I'm sure he has,' she said emphatically. She hesitated again, and then carried on as lightly as she could. 'Anyway, I gather the village seems to feel that I'd have got what I wanted, one way or another.'

He smiled at her. 'Have they written you in as the villainess already?'

She nodded, flushing, and he asked, 'How do you know?'

'Oh, Tilly told us. It's probably what she came up to say,' she replied evenly.

'There are always plenty of people to tell you what's being said about you when it isn't pleasant,' he reassured her.

'Yes, I know, and you soon hear what's being said in a place like this anyway,' she agreed.

He considered her for a moment. 'Miss Rossington, a little while ago you said that Mr Rother was afraid that your tea visitors might damage the priory buildings. Did he have reason to think that?' She looked at him, puzzled, and he elaborated, 'Had he found some damage in the past that made him worry about more being done?'

Lucy shook her head immediately. 'No, definitely not. We would soon have heard about it. There's never been anything like that here. Who would do it?'

'You've taken the words out of my mouth,' he said. 'We've found what looks like some fresh damage to the buildings.

Nothing much,' he added hastily as she frowned, 'but I would like all of you to take a look at it and see what you think.'

'Alright. Now?'

'No, we'll go down together when the statements have been taken. Do you have any idea who might have done the damage?'

'No,' she replied at once, 'I can't think of anyone who would do it. There aren't any petty vandals around here.'

'Do you know who could have attacked Mr Rother?'

'No,' she sounded frustrated, 'we've thought and thought, but really we can't think of anyone who'd want to hurt him.'

'And where were you between one and three o'clock this morning?'

She smiled. 'In bed, and sound asleep, I'm afraid.'

'Did you hear anything?'

'No, I slept right through the night. I usually do. But I don't expect the attack made much noise.' She stiffened as a thought struck her. 'Would Graham have had time to cry out?'

'We can't tell yet. He was probably caught unawares and didn't have time to call,' he said soberly, and she shivered, suddenly picturing the scene.

'Which way does your bedroom face?' he asked her.

'Towards the front. I have the room above the porch. Gran has the west room and Will the east. The other rooms are all used for guests.'

His brows drew together thoughtfully. 'I've spoken to your grandmother about seeing over the house. Would you be able to take me round later on?' The sergeant glanced up from his notebook in surprise, but returned immediately to his scribbling.

'Of course, whenever you want to go,' Lucy said.

'Do any of the rooms overlook the priory, or the track to it?'

'No,' she smiled. 'It was never a picturesque ruin, and my ancestors were far too practical, and poor, to alter the house for the sake of a mere view.' Her smile faded, and she added reflectively, 'At least, Will's room is above this one and has windows in the same places,' she gestured around her, 'so to an extent he can see the track from the front drive that runs round the back of the estate office. That's the way Graham probably walked from the lodge to the priory. The courtyards are too full of jumble for him to come through from the gatehouse in the dark.'

'I see,' the inspector said slowly, 'but you don't think there would be a view of the priory buildings from Will's room?'

'I'm sure there isn't,' she said at once. 'You can see the tops of the buildings of course, but nothing lower down because of the bushes.'

He changed the subject. 'Are you aware of the estate matters that Mr Rother deals with?'

'Yes, at least I'm learning a bit about them. I didn't bother in the past, but Graham is quite happy to put me in the picture. He knows every detail of the place and,' Lucy observed, 'he's a good instructor.'

'Is there anything in connection with the estate that could have provoked this kind of attack? Anybody he might have upset?'

Lucy pondered for a while, and then shook her head. 'No. Many of the farms are empty, there's little profit in farming these days, and all the others are run by long-term tenants. And there are no new issues. Only things like repairs, and however impassioned discussions about roofs and barns may become, they aren't going to result in tenants creeping round the old priory at night, on the off-chance that Graham will come out to have his head bashed.'

He smiled at her suddenly. 'Thank you. You've been very helpful. If you should think of anything else that may be useful, anything at all however small, please let us know at once.'

Lucy got to her feet. 'Yes, of course I will. We must find out who did it. Poor old Graham deserves that at least, although I can't help wondering if perhaps he disturbed a tramp.'

'That's possible, of course,' the inspector said noncommittally. He hesitated, and then continued, 'But you should bear in mind that the attacker may be someone you know, and that they could be very dangerous.'

Lucy's face was sober. 'I shan't forget, however incredible it seems.' She turned and began to cross the room to the door which the sergeant was holding open for her.

The inspector spoke again and she stopped, turning to look at him. 'One moment, Miss Rossington. Your grandmother mentioned somebody to whom you gave permission to use a metal detector in the grounds. Can you tell me his name?'

'Yes, of course. It's Simon Trent. He was just leaving as you arrived.' The inspector nodded. 'He's a potter and he lives at the Old Wheelwright's cottage in the village. He wouldn't be around at night, but I suppose he may have noticed something odd at other times.'

'You can never tell,' the inspector agreed. 'How did Mr Rother feel about him operating in the grounds?'

'Oh, he was furious,' Lucy admitted blithely. 'But he's coming round; he's really very interested in some of the things Simon's found.'

He looked at her silently for a few seconds before asking, 'Have you had any other visitors in the last few weeks?'

She reflected. 'Anna Evesleigh from Moreton House has been over a few times. She's an old friend, and she's at home for a bit. And,' she added blandly, 'Tilly Barlow has been in and out. She's been doing some signs for me. Her cottage is in the village too. Honeysuckle Cottage, you'll recognise it by the gnomes in the garden.' The sergeant smothered a chuckle and there was amusement in Inspector Elliot's grey eyes. 'Oh, and of course there's Mike Shannon, the man that Hugh contacted about the priory. I don't know much about him, but I expect Hugh can tell you anything you want to know.'

'Yes, I'm sure he can,' the inspector said. 'Would you ask your brother to come in next, please?'

Lucy smiled. 'Of course. He's hardly been able to wait for

his turn.'

As Sergeant Peters shut the door behind her Inspector Elliot returned to his seat. He stared in front of him, frowning a little, and occasionally making a note on the pad of paper in front of him. He looked up suddenly. 'Well, Tom, what do you make of it so far?'

The sergeant was sitting on his hard chair again, and he leaned forward, placing his large red hands on his bulky knees. 'Well, sir,' he ruminated, 'it seems to me the young lady may have the right of it. An old tramp, or even a young one, with a bit too much drink on board.'

The inspector was still frowning. 'A possibility, of course, but would a drunken tramp bother to drag his victim into the bushes and try to set up an accident? Surely he'd be more likely to bolt when he saw what he'd done?'

'Yes, that's true, unless maybe he'd an idea of putting off the finding of the victim to give himself a bit of time.'

'Yes, possible, but not really likely, I think. Nonetheless, make a note to look into reports of tramps about here.' He sat, his brows still knitted, until the sergeant ventured a question.

'You're not thinking, sir, that it'll be somebody from the manor?'

'No, Tom, I think it's unlikely, if you consider what we know about the attack.' He picked up a pencil and absently twirled it between his fingers. 'Firstly, the assailant will probably be taller than Mr Rother to have been able to inflict the first blow, and that disbars everyone from the manor. There is, of course, the possibility that one of them stood on the pile of rubble there, but I think that would be a bit precarious.'

He twiddled the pencil again. 'Secondly, we know the assailant was alone, or at least carried out the attack on their own.' The sergeant stared at him, thinking about this. 'Look, Tom, Rother was dragged along the grass to the place where he was dumped. If there was more than one person involved in the attack Rother would have been carried – much easier and faster.

And as far as the household here are concerned, I shouldn't think any of them would have the strength to drag a man of his weight that distance. '

The sergeant nodded, and the inspector looked up as a loud knocking sounded on the door. 'You'd better let the boy in before he batters it down.'

The sergeant trod heavily to the door and opened it upon Will, who had one hand raised to beat another tattoo on the panels. The other grasped Hades firmly by the collar. 'I say,' Will demanded anxiously, 'would you mind if I brought Hades in with me? He'll be very good. It's just that Gran doesn't want him with her and Juno in the hall, and Hades will scratch the door down if I leave him in the scullery alone.'

The inspector eyed the big black dog, who gazed at him hopefully. 'Alright, bring him in, but only if you can keep him quiet.'

'Thanks very much,' Will said gratefully, taking the chair in front of the desk that the sergeant indicated. He pushed Hades down and rested his feet on the dog's woolly back. He settled himself more comfortably on the chair and waited expectantly, while the sergeant resumed his place with a grin on his face.

The inspector looked across the table at Will and smiled encouragingly. 'Will, I've been through things with your grandmother and your sister, and now I would like to hear what you've got to say. But we'd better start off with the routine questions.'

Will nodded eagerly. 'Okay.'

'Where were you between one and three o'clock this morning?' the inspector asked gravely.

'In bed,' Will responded dismally. 'I didn't hear a thing either. I'd been thinking of going out to watch for the barn owl, too. I just wish I had.'

The inspector kept his thoughts to himself. 'Do you know of anyone who might have wanted to attack Mr Rother?' he continued.

'No, of course not,' Will said. 'He can be a real bore at times, and a bit of a drag too, but you don't bash people on the head for that. At least,' he amended thoughtfully, 'I should think that if you do, you'd do it when they were being a bore or a drag, not get away from them and then come back, hanging round to bash them in revenge.'

The inspector disentangled this speech, forbearing to glance at the sergeant to see how he was getting it down in his note-book. 'I should think you're right. You can't think of any other reason why he might be attacked, somebody he might have upset more seriously?'

'No, Graham doesn't upset people like that. I mean, he doesn't go in for rows and fights, or things like that. And he doesn't go away from here for anything either, he's always doing something on the estate.'

'But I understood that he'd had, umm, a disagreement with your sister,' the inspector said coolly.

Will flushed angrily and clenched his fists. Hades struggled to sit up, and he told him sharply, 'Stay!' He glared across the desk at the inspector. 'That's nonsense. They disagreed, okay, they were always disagreeing about things. But then so do I.' He clarified this at once. 'I mean, I disagree with Graham and I disagree with Lucy about all sorts of things, but that doesn't mean we go around bashing each other on the head.'

'Do any of you ever agree about anything?' the inspector asked in some amusement.

'Oh yes,' Will said readily. 'We agree much more often than you might think. In fact, I agreed with Graham only the other day.'

'Oh?' the inspector said encouragingly, ignoring the sound of Hades chewing vigorously at one of Will's shoes.

'Yes, I did,' Will said. 'Stop it, Hades.' He pulled his foot away and poked it in the dog's side, so that Hades wagged his tail vigorously, hoping that there was going to be a game at last. 'I didn't think Lucy should let Simon go around with his rotten metal detector. We don't want him here all the time.'

'I see,' said the inspector, who did. 'You don't like him?'

'No,' Will said emphatically, 'I don't. He's a bit of a wimp, what with his pots and his bits of nails.'

'Nails?' queried the inspector, fascinated.

'That's what he normally finds with his detector,' Will explained. 'Rusty old nails and bits of horseshoes. Anna went out detecting with him, but she didn't stay long,' he said with satisfaction, and then his face clouded over. 'Mind you, I think Graham's coming round because Simon found an old fish trap, or something he said was an old fish trap. I can't see how anyone could tell what it was, it just looked like twisted bits of old metal. Anyhow, I heard Graham tell Lucy that maybe the detecting might be useful after all, because Simon might find something interesting. Something else interesting!' He emphasised this with disgust. 'I can't think what he expects Simon to find though, unless he really does believe in the prior's treasure.'

The sergeant lifted his head which had been bent over his notepad while he scribbled furiously, and the inspector leaned forward. 'The prior's treasure? What's that?' he asked.

'Oh, it doesn't exist really. It's just a story, like the one about the monks walking on the anniversary of their expulsion,' Will said disgustedly.

'Well, what is the story?' the inspector persisted patiently.

'I don't know when it started,' Will recited the legend in a deadpan tone, 'but the priory was supposed to have gone downhill before the closure. The monks had been selling off the valuables, but the prior was said to have kept the best things of all and hidden them before the King's Commissioners came.'

He stopped, but continued reluctantly when the inspector nodded encouragingly. 'Well, apparently he tried to come back for them, but was found dead, murdered, on the cliff path.' He gestured vaguely behind him. Hades created a diversion at this moment by squirming out from under Will's feet, and bringing one of his back paws up for a good scratch at his ear.

'Were many monks expelled from the priory?' the inspector asked.

'No, there weren't many left. Six, I think, with the prior. No, five, because one died just after the Commissioners came. He was the last one to be buried here. I don't know where the prior was buried,' he finished dispassionately, and then his eyes lit up gleefully.

'Tilly's been on about having a ghost hunt, you know, because she's latched on to this story about the monks walking. She reckons it's because the last monk wasn't buried properly, or some rot like that. Anyhow, Graham won't like it, and I bet we'll be able to put her off for good now.'

'Had it been arranged?' Inspector Elliot pursued these strands of information diligently, somewhat to the sergeant's surprise.

'No, Lucy had already put her off, but she'd have kept on about it, you know,' Will explained frankly.

The inspector reverted to the earlier topic and asked, 'Is there any foundation to the story of the treasure?'

'No, I shouldn't think so. Gran doesn't believe it, and I should think if there had been anything to discover one of my ancestors would have found it.' Will stared at the inspector, suddenly alert. 'Why? Do you think Graham was looking for it? I don't think he believed in it either, although he liked the story. Anyway, even if he did, he could look for it at any time, he wouldn't need to search during the night.'

'Can you think of any reason why somebody might want to damage the priory buildings?' The inspector changed the subject, deeming that it could continue for some time.

'No, who'd want to come out here to scribble on a few old stones?' Will was scornful, and then sat up straight. 'Do you mean somebody has?' he demanded.

The inspector nodded. 'Not very much damage done, but it looks fresh. I'd like you all to come down and take a look at it later.'

'I should say we'll want to look at it,' Will said. 'Who on

earth…' He broke off abruptly and stared at the inspector. 'That's why Graham was attacked,' he said, his voice rising in excitement. 'He found somebody damaging the priory, and they went for him. Gosh! Who'd have thought it?'

His excitement faded as the inspector answered calmly, 'We've thought of that, of course, but it doesn't take us any closer to who might have been there and what they were doing.'

'No, I suppose not.' Will replied reluctantly. 'But I'll bet that's how it happened.'

'Perhaps,' the inspector said blandly, watching Hades sniffing hopefully at the sergeant's trouser pockets. 'Have you seen anything suspicious in or around the ruins?'

Will considered briefly. 'No, I haven't and we'd soon notice anything that was different.'

'Yes, I should think you would. I don't expect you have many visitors in the area either?'

'None that I know of. Yet, that is,' he grinned suddenly, and Hades pushed his wet nose meaningfully onto the inspector's knee. Inspector Elliot absently began to rub the big dog's ears and Hades closed his eyes in bliss. His master continued, 'If Lucy's schemes come off there may be plenty soon.'

'But are they going to come off?' the inspector enquired. 'I understand that Mr Rother disapproves of them.'

'He came round in the end. Oh, do you mean Mike's ideas?'

'I believe I do, if he's the man Mr Carey sent down.'

'Well, I don't think Hugh sent him exactly, more that he mentioned the place to him and Mike came zooming down. He's the sort who zooms around all the time, I should think.' He smiled reminiscently.

The inspector noticed the smile and commented, 'You like him.'

'He's okay. He's wild about this place, and I bet he'll get things done. And boy,' Will added with satisfaction, 'you should have heard him squash Anna.'

'Anna?'

'Anna Evesleigh. She's a friend of Lucy's and her father lives just outside the village. When she stays with him she's always over here, draping herself about the place. Darling this and darling that,' he said scornfully. 'Simon's a sucker and even Hugh puts up with her, but he already knew her in London so he probably can't avoid her.'

A smothered sound from the back of the room drew the inspector's sardonic gaze to Sergeant Peters, who was muffling a sudden fit of coughing with a large white handkerchief. The inspector continued imperturbably with his questions, although his lips twitched. 'You don't seem to regard Mr Carey as a visitor?'

'Hugh? Of course not. I suppose he hasn't been here for long, but it seems as though we've known him for ages. He's a naturalist, you know, like my father, only Hugh is interested in our birds and animals and things, not just foreign ones. He's a barrister too, but I didn't know that.'

'Oh?' The inspector interrupted without compunction. 'I thought you'd retained his services?'

'We have. At least, I asked him to help us, but I didn't know then that he was a barrister.'

'Did he tell you?' the inspector asked.

'No, it seems Gran knew, because she'd followed some case he'd been involved in.' A thought struck him. 'Anna must have known too, but I suppose she's forgotten; she's rather dim.'

'We're getting a bit away from the point,' the inspector said. 'How does Mr Rother feel about all these plans Mr Shannon is putting forward?'

'Well, there aren't any plans as such, you know,' Will explained. 'Mike was only here for a few hours, but he said all sorts of things were possible. It was very exciting, but I think in some ways we were a bit dazed at first, so we've really only got ideas at the moment. Although I don't expect it will be long before there are plans of all sorts; Lucy doesn't hang around, and there are some things I think it will be worth doing, too.'

'Did Mr Rother express his views about these ideas?' the inspector persisted.

'Well, he got excited too when Mike was here. I think he was a bit cross at first, but then he got interested in what Mike said. But afterwards he didn't say much about it, and the rest of us were talking about nothing else, you know,' he said ingenuously.

'We, that is Lucy and I, think that he was probably worried about it all by then, because he never liked things being done to the priory. I can't see why he was upset about this though, because if Mike's ideas work out we'll know a lot more about the place, and the buildings might be restored. You'd have thought he'd be pleased,' the boy said, puzzled, and then his brow cleared.

'I expect he will be when it's all sorted out, and he's had time to think it over. When he's better, of course.' Will had optimistically overcome his earlier fears for Graham, and did not notice the quick look Sergeant Peters cast at the inspector. The boy continued, 'He doesn't really like things to change, but he always comes round in the end.'

'Is there anything else you can add?' the inspector asked. 'Anything you've noticed or heard that might be relevant?'

Will answered at once, 'No, I've thought and thought, and there's just nothing at all. It's such a weird thing to have happened, but of course Graham may have seen the person who hit him, and he'll be able to tell you when he comes round.' The silence impinged upon his consciousness and he stared at the inspector. 'He is going to be alright, isn't he?'

'I'm sure the hospital will let us know at once if he's able to talk to us,' the inspector said quietly, and stood up. 'I've already said to your sister and I must make it clear to you, Will, that the attacker may be somebody you know and they could be dangerous.' Will's eyes widened with excitement and the inspector continued, stressing his words carefully. 'If you think of or notice anything else at all, you must come and tell me at once. Don't try to do anything about it. Will you do that?'

Will nodded emphatically and the inspector smiled, bending down to stroke Hades, who was now snuffling round his shoes with interest. 'Well then, that's all. I'm going to see Mr Rother's nephew next. Can you listen for his departure, and then ask Mr Carey to come and see me.'

'Okay,' the boy said, grabbing a reluctant Hades and pulling him out of the room.

Inspector Elliot turned to the sergeant. 'I hope you got all that down, Tom,' he said blandly.

'I did, sir, and enjoyed every bit of it,' the sergeant responded robustly. 'Not much that youngster will miss, I reckon, and as frank as his sister.'

'Yes,' the inspector concurred, 'they both seem to be very straightforward. A difficult situation for them, being left with this property hanging on their hands.'

'They seem to care a fair bit about it, too,' the sergeant sounded puzzled.

'More than they'd expected to, I think,' the inspector said. 'Well, what do you make of it now?'

The sergeant rubbed his chin with one large hand while he pondered. 'I suppose there can't be anything in the boy's story of the treasure?' he asked slowly.

The inspector frowned, absently picking up the pencil again and twirling it between his fingers. 'Unlikely, I should think, and besides, the story has been known for a long time. It seems to me that the new factor in this business is Mike Shannon and his ideas about the priory.'

'Yes,' said the sergeant doubtfully. 'But why should anybody be worried about them?'

'That,' said the inspector, 'is what we must try to find out. In the meantime, you'd better go and get the nephew.'

He sat back in the chair, twiddling the pencil and thinking deeply. The sound of heavy footsteps in the corridor alerted him, and he looked up to see Jack coming through the doorway.

'About time too,' he said sharply. 'I want to get over to the hospital as soon as I can.'

'I'm sure you do,' the inspector agreed amiably. 'We'll try not to keep you long.'

'Huh!' Jack grunted, sitting uninvited in the chair in front of the desk. 'So just what has been going on?'

'It will be easier if I ask you the questions,' Inspector Elliot responded evenly. 'Starting with your full name please.'

'Jack Correll,' the other man snapped.

The inspector's eyes narrowed very slightly, before he continued. 'Where you were between one and three o'clock this morning?'

Jack looked back at him coldly. 'I can't see what that has to do with you.'

The inspector considered him thoughtfully. 'Your uncle has been very seriously injured,' he said deliberately. 'It looked as though it was an accident, but there is some reason to doubt that.' He noted Jack's scowl, and continued, 'So you can see we're interested in what everyone was doing this morning.'

Jack stared at him belligerently. 'I can't see why, when the village gossips already have a pretty good idea of what happened,' he said rudely. 'I should have thought you'd only need to talk to this lot.' He jerked his head towards the rest of the house, and added with a spurt of malice, 'Even if they didn't actually see to the poor old devil, they're responsible anyway. The whole place is crumbling, so it wouldn't be at all surprising if a stone has fallen on him.'

'How do you know that's what happened?' the inspector asked quietly.

Jack was startled. 'I don't know. Somebody told me, one of them I expect,' he gestured in the direction of the sitting room.

The inspector studied him for a few seconds, until Jack felt impelled to speak again. 'Well, alright, I went into Corrington last night for a spot of life. It's fairly deadly here,' he said disparagingly. 'They're all safely shut away in their little homes by midnight.'

'Where did you go in Corrington?'

'Oh, some club in the city centre. Downstairs near the shops, lots of lights.'

The inspector thought of the number of places that would fit the description. 'We'll ask round,' he said levelly. 'Were you there all night?'

'Well, ah, no,' Jack smiled disarmingly. 'I met a nice little number there, and went back to her place. That's why I didn't get back until this morning.'

'Her name?' the inspector asked flatly.

'I'm not sure,' Jack said. 'Janey, I think.' He added helpfully, 'Lots of blonde hair.'

'That's not really very informative, Mr Correll. If you think of more details, it would be useful.'

'Of course. I'll see what I can come up with.' Jack checked his watch, and began to get to his feet. 'Can I get off now?'

'Shortly.' The inspector saw the look of displeasure on the other man's face as he sank back onto his chair. 'Why are you in the area if you find it so dull?'

'Visiting Uncle Graham, of course,' Jack replied promptly.

'Are you a frequent visitor?'

Jack smiled without humour. 'Inspector, I'm sure you've been told by them,' he nodded again towards the sitting room, 'that I hardly ever darken my uncle's doorstep.'

'So why are you here now?'

'Family feeling,' he retorted. 'After all, he is getting on a bit. And,' he added, 'I had a faint forlorn hope that it wasn't as dull here as I remembered.'

'I see.' The inspector appraised him again, and then said abruptly, 'You can go now, but please don't leave the area.' As Jack stood up, the inspector asked, 'Where will you be staying?'

Jack looked at him in surprise. 'In the lodge, of course. I won't leave until Uncle Graham is alright again.'

'Of course,' the inspector responded evenly. 'You'll have to wait until the officers are finished there.'

'And when is that likely to be?' Jack demanded.

'I'm not really sure. Perhaps you should ring me from the hospital.'

'Very well.' He turned and stalked out of the room.

Inspector Elliot stared after him for a while, and then turned to his sergeant. 'Very interesting, didn't you think, Tom?'

'Doesn't like the Rossingtons, does he, sir?' the sergeant said with a grin.

'He made that very clear,' the inspector agreed. 'And he's provided a very obvious alibi, one he thinks will be hard to check, I suspect.' He looked up at a knock on the door. 'Ah, that will be Carey. Let him in, please.'

SIX

The inspector came round the desk to greet Hugh as he entered the room. 'Take a seat and tell me what you know about this business,' he invited.

Hugh sat back in the chair and crossed his legs in a leisurely fashion. 'Well, I'm not sure that I can throw much light on the matter. There are certainly no concrete facts or obvious suspects to offer you, if that's what you're hoping for.'

The inspector shrugged, undismayed. 'I hope for something of the sort in every case I investigate, but I've never come across much in that line yet.'

Hugh smiled. 'I'd be out of work if it happened too often.'

The inspector's eyebrows rose in simulated surprise. 'But I thought you were following a new career. Naturalist, isn't it?'

'The two aren't mutually exclusive,' Hugh said. 'I've got to the stage where I can pick my cases, and that's what I intend to do. It gives me time to explore other fields of interest – writing, photography, maybe even publishing.'

'Seriously?' the inspector sounded astounded.

'Yes, I've even got a couple of commissions for pictures with accompanying texts.'

'Not bad,' the inspector commented, with a touch of envy. 'You're a lucky man.'

'Would you give it all up if you could?' Hugh asked him curiously.

The inspector thought about this, and then his eyes twinkled. 'There are plenty of times when I'd say yes to that, but if it came to the crunch, no I wouldn't, not entirely. But it would be good to have the best of both worlds.'

'It is,' Hugh said. 'Try it.'

'Given the opportunity, I probably will,' the inspector said. 'But back to the police work now. Nobody seems to know of any reason why Mr Rother was attacked. Do you?'

Hugh's answer was just as blunt. 'No. The man is a bit of a bore, but I should think that's the worst anybody could say of him. He's good at his job, an innocuous chap in all ways as far as I can tell, albeit more than a touch obsessive about this place.'

'Do you think the plans, present or future, for the priory had anything to do with the attack?'

Hugh reflected. 'I don't really see how they can have. Equally, Mike's ideas are the only new element in the matter, as far as I can tell. The people most obviously involved in that, apart from Mike, are the Rossingtons, and I really can't envisage any of them coming to blows with Graham over it.' The inspector was silent and Hugh looked across the desk at him in some surprise. 'Do you regard them as suspects?'

He shook his head slowly. 'Not seriously, not as strong ones, but you know I can't rule them out entirely at this stage.'

'True,' Hugh conceded, 'but you can bear in mind that they're all used to Graham and have never had any doubts of their ability to handle him.'

'Speed might have been of the essence,' the inspector offered reluctantly.

Hugh snorted. 'It wasn't,' he said shortly. 'Why should it be? Mike's ideas are only at the suggestion stage. I imagine that it would be some time before any detailed plans could be made. But you can ask him that for yourself, he'll be down sometime today.'

The inspector's eyes widened and Hugh explained smoothly,

'He doesn't let the grass grow under his feet. He rang me last night to demand accommodation for an indefinite period, but I doubt that he'll know anything about this business yet, unless it's already hit the papers.'

'No, not yet,' the inspector said. 'It may be in the evening editions. What time did he ring you?'

'Just after midnight. He'd been trying earlier, but I'd been out to dinner with Anna.' He read the query in Inspector Elliot's eyes. 'True, but Anna had to be home early. She's coddling her father. I dropped her at her door at about eleven-thirty, and came back to Roscombe as I was toying with the idea of going out bat watching. I'd been in collecting my gear for about ten minutes when Mike rang, and he must have been on the phone for at least twenty minutes, enthusing over the priory. When he finally rang off I decided against going out again.' He smiled blandly at the inspector. 'The sky had clouded over and, anyway, late nights are common when Mike's around, so I thought I'd get some sleep while I could.'

The inspector did not comment on this, but asked, 'Anna would be Miss Evesleigh? The boy mentioned her.'

Hugh smiled suddenly. 'I'm sure he did. He's a bit young to appreciate the attraction yet, but you'll see for yourself.'

The inspector nodded. 'I shall. You dropped her at Moreton House. Did you see her go in?'

'Of course.' Hugh paused. 'At least, come to think of it, I saw her open the door, but she waved me off so I didn't actually see her step over the threshold.' His lips twitched. 'Even Will wouldn't credit Anna with a sudden urge to attack Graham, and,' he added, 'I can't think of any reason why she should come over here later to wander in the grounds.'

The inspector's face was expressionless. 'Did you come through the village on your way home?'

'Yes. I don't have to, the approach to my cottage is along the farm track, but I went down to the harbour.' He shrugged. 'I'd no real reason to, I just like the sea in moonlight and I wanted to judge what the weather was like.'

'Did you notice anybody about?' the inspector asked.

'No, they generally all go early to bed around here. There weren't even any lights on, except in the pub.' He grinned at the inspector, and then added, 'Oh, and in the potter's cottage. I thought I caught sight of a light in his studio too.' Hugh paused, and then went on evenly, 'He was up here this morning and he mentioned that he'd been firing some work last night.'

'Ah well, maybe he saw somebody around.' The inspector said philosophically. 'Would he have any reason to be involved himself?'

'Only through this business about the metal detecting, and I can't see why it should escalate into violence. No,' he continued, 'nothing else that I've been able to think of.' The inspector glanced at him sharply, and Hugh met his eyes calmly. 'I imagine it would have been difficult for a woman to attack and move Graham. That rather narrows the field.'

'You're assuming it's somebody local?' the inspector asked quickly.

'Not exclusively. Until the reason for the attack ..., no,' Hugh corrected himself, 'the presence of the attacker in the priory is explained, I can't see how we can do more than guess at identities.'

'If it was a man who attacked Mr Rother, would you exclude the possibility of a woman being present?'

Hugh looked thoughtful. 'No,' he said slowly, 'I don't think so, but surely the fact that Graham was dragged rather than carried to the bushes must indicate that the man was alone.'

'Not necessarily,' the inspector said. 'We can't exclude the possibility that any partner who was there, man or woman, may have panicked.'

Hugh considered this. 'Yes,' he said evenly, 'that must be a possibility, but it can only be conjecture at the moment.'

'How seriously are you representing the family?' The inspector threw out the question sharply.

Hugh smiled faintly. 'I'm around if they want me. I can't imagine that any of them will be genuinely in need of my services, but this business is likely to put them under a lot of strain, and there's a fair amount for them to worry about anyway, with this place.'

The inspector commented, 'You seem to be well accepted, almost a member of the family yourself.'

'Not entirely,' Hugh said blandly.

'Oh?' The inspector was interested. 'I thought you went down well all round.'

'I suspect Lucy wouldn't agree,' he said ruefully.

'Famous charm fails at last?' queried the inspector sardonically.

'Resisted, at least,' Hugh conceded. 'I believe she resents my involvement in what she regards as her responsibilities. She's used to fending for herself and doesn't relish assistance, even when she needs it. She can be a stubborn little fool at times,' he said in sudden exasperation.

The inspector was about to speak, but after a quick interested look at Hugh's face he held his tongue. 'Well, unless there's anything else you can tell me, we'll take you all down to look at the priory.'

'Why?' asked Hugh.

'Some damage done to the walls that I want your comments on,' the inspector replied briefly.

Hugh frowned, but resisted an urge to question him. 'Fine. Graham showed me around a few days ago, so I'm pretty certain I'd spot anything fresh.' He hesitated, and then made up his mind. 'He mentioned then that he thought strangers might have been in the priory buildings from time to time.'

The inspector straightened abruptly. 'What! Nobody has mentioned this.'

'I don't think he told anybody else. Partly, he didn't want to worry the family or, more likely, stir them up. Partly, it was a very nebulous feeling, based on finding the odd unexplained cigarette stub.'

Inspector Elliot was watching him closely. 'And?'

'Nothing much. When I was exploring one of the caves in Rosgully Cove, I found a passage leading out and up, and there was another cigarette stub in it.' He looked levelly at the inspector.

'Local lads having a bit of fun?' he questioned.

'Perhaps, and yet the Rossingtons don't know about the passage.'

Inspector Elliot frowned. 'Then how did you find it?' he demanded.

'I used to do a lot of caving, and you get a feel for the shape of the rock. This passage is pretty high up and not visible from the cave floor, so I don't think it would be found casually.'

The inspector sat thoughtfully twiddling his pencil. He decided suddenly and leaned forward. 'Look, Carey, this could be important, as perhaps you've guessed.' By the door the sergeant looked startled.

'We've reason to believe there's a wide network involved in people smuggling.' His mouth narrowed. 'It's all very cleverly done. A ship with its human cargo is met by small boats at different points along the south coast, and just a small part of that cargo is offloaded into each one.' He looked grimly at Hugh. 'You can guess how it is. We can identify the ships, but we don't have all of the land-based players yet, and when we throw out our net we want to gather in as many of them as we can.'

He paused, and Hugh waited in silence until he continued. 'We don't know of any trail in this area, but it's just possible that this tunnel may be involved, and the old priory buildings could then be a staging post.' His face tightened. 'And of course that blows the whole case here much wider open.'

He looked at Hugh appraisingly. 'You did suspect something, didn't you?'

'Yes,' Hugh admitted, 'although I'm not sure why. Perhaps because Graham isn't at all a fanciful man and he clearly did believe somebody had been in the priory.' He shrugged. 'And then somebody mentioned the smugglers' caves, and I was just curious. An occupational failing, Elliot, putting together a theory and testing it.'

'Hmm,' the inspector said. 'But you do realise that this must involve at least one local, don't you?'

'Yes, and in a dangerous game. The sooner it's sorted the better,' Hugh said sternly.

'Quite,' the inspector agreed. 'Do let me know if you formulate any more theories.'

'I will,' Hugh promised. 'Do you want me to say anything about this to the Rossingtons?'

The inspector hesitated. 'Damnation, I don't know,' he said heavily. 'I suppose they should be warned, if you can trust them to keep their mouths shut.'

'Yes, I'm sure they will,' Hugh said. 'And now, shall we gather your party and go to inspect the damage?'

The inspector said to the sergeant, 'Ask the others to meet us in the hall, will you?' He turned to Hugh as the sergeant left the room. 'Rother's nephew. Ever met him before?' he demanded.

Hugh looked surprised. 'No, I don't think so, although,' his brows drew together, 'he did seem familiar when he arrived. But he's similar in some ways to his uncle.'

'Even more similar to his father,' Inspector Elliot said bluntly. 'Edward Correll.'

Hugh stood very still, then gave a low whistle. 'Well, well,' he said softly, 'so there's three of us from the Benton case here now.' His lips twisted. 'So that's why I'm such a figure of hate.'

'What do you mean?' the inspector queried sharply.

'Nothing much. It just explains some of the venom in his comments.'

The inspector frowned. 'This case becomes more serious by the minute. Can you be sure that the Rossington youngsters would tell me anything they know?'

'Yes,' Hugh responded instantly, 'I'm sure they would.

They're shocked by what's happened, and it's made them realise how much Graham means to them. They'll do whatever they can to help catch his attacker.'

Hugh considered the inspector for a second. 'You think he's dangerous?'

Inspector Elliot scowled. 'You know the answer to that as well as I do. Even if our wider suspicions are unfounded, I think the attack was unpremeditated, and I suspect that the attacker is now a very frightened person. You know what frightened people can be capable of too.' Hugh's mouth tightened and the inspector started to say, 'And he'll be even more frightened if ...' but broke off as the sergeant returned. Hugh looked at him quickly, but did not press him to finish.

It was only a short walk across the prior's bridge, past the policeman who briskly saluted the inspector, past the little path through the bushes where Graham had been found that morning, past the ruined night stairs where patches of ground were marked off and covered with plastic sheeting. Then they stood in the old cloisters, a sombre silent group gazing in blank astonishment at the damaged walls.

The inspector waited patiently, studying their faces as they looked around them.

'What on earth was he doing?' Will burst out. 'It looks as though he was trying to make windows!'

Hugh stepped forward, glancing at the inspector who nodded slightly, and fingered the damage. 'These stones have been chiselled out of the wall,' he said, touching the edge of a small hole. 'But why?' He was almost talking to himself, but the others listened intently. 'At regular spaces all along this wall. And the others?' he queried suddenly, turning to the inspector, who shook his head silently. 'Ah, this is where he was interrupted. Look, you can see where he'd started to chip at the mortar.'

'That must have been when Graham came along,' Will said soberly. 'Boy, wouldn't he have been wild to see this?'

'Yes,' said his grandmother, 'yes, he'd have been beside himself.'

Lucy did not comment, but was gazing around picturing the scene, her face very white. Hugh said impatiently, 'It wouldn't have been quite as you're suggesting. Graham didn't get this far, he didn't see any of this.' The Rossingtons looked at him in surprise.

'Well,' he said sharply, 'use your brains. You know where he was struck down.'

'Of course,' Lucy said, 'he was in the gateway. Whoever hit him had already heard him coming, so they snatched up a lump of stone from the rubble and waited in the shadow of the arch.' She swallowed hard. 'Graham didn't see any of this.' She glanced at Hugh, adding quietly, 'He probably didn't even see who hit him.'

'That may be true,' Hugh said, as the inspector opened his mouth to interrupt, 'but none of you will you say so to anybody else.'

Lucy looked at him indignantly, antagonism showing in her face, but before she could utter the words brimming on her tongue a uniformed policeman appeared in the archway. He came up to the group and with a muttered apology drew the inspector to one side to whisper briefly in his ear.

The inspector dismissed him with a short word of thanks and turned to the waiting group, his eyes meeting Hugh's pointedly for a second. 'The hospital has been in touch. I'm sorry,' he looked round at their strained waiting faces, 'Mr Rother has just died.' His eyes again met Hugh's fleetingly, and as he read the question in them he shook his head slightly.

Nobody moved. Lucy stood frozen to the spot, while unaccustomed tears sprang into Isobel Rossington's eyes. It was Will who broke the silence. His jaws worked for a moment, and then he blurted out, 'So you're looking for a murderer. The man who attacked Graham is a murderer now.'

Lucy made an involuntary motion of rejection, quickly stopped, and Hugh replied deliberately, 'Yes, Will, a murderer. A dangerous, and possibly frightened, person.' As he finished speaking he glanced briefly at the inspector. 'We'll go back to the house.'

He ushered them through the archway, and they walked slowly and heavily back along the track. Lucy stumbled once as they passed the thick bushes, but quickly regained her balance, so that Hugh drew back his proffered hand unnoticed.

'If you're going, then I'll come too,' Will said firmly.

Lucy looked affectionately across the kitchen at him. 'Fine, we'll go together. I could do with somebody to carry the shopping back.'

They walked slowly down the rear drive, Will swinging the shopping basket backwards and forwards. Neither of them spoke for some time until Will said, glancing at his sister's face, 'Lucy, do you have any idea who killed Graham?'

She took a while to answer. 'No, Will, I don't,' she said, and paused meditatively. 'At first I didn't really believe that anyone could have attacked him, but now, well, now I find I'm considering everyone. It's horrible,' she finished vehemently.

Will nodded. 'Yes, I know. But perhaps it's best, because I can't see that it could be somebody from outside.'

'It's still possible that it was, because it's so senseless to think that somebody here attacked him. Somebody we know. Who? And why now?'

'Do you think Hugh knows something?' he asked doubtfully.

Lucy turned to him in surprise. 'Hugh? Why should he?'

'Oh, I don't know,' Will said vaguely. 'I just thought he seemed a bit preoccupied.'

'Well, it's enough to preoccupy anybody,' Lucy pointed out.

Will opened his mouth to say something more, but shut it again as he realised they were approaching the village shop. He mounted the steps and pushed open the door of a crowded little room. Almost every inch of space inside was used, leaving a narrow circuit in the centre around shelves stacked high with packets and tins of food. Fishing nets, buckets, brooms and plant canes hung from hooks in the rafters, tapping taller customers on the head. Crates of vegetables were stacked along the walls, crowding boxes of shoes and boots into untidy piles in the far corners.

Today the tiny room was also full almost to overflowing with people, mainly women but with a sprinkling of older men too. The agitated buzz of conversation stopped abruptly as Lucy stepped into the room, followed by Will, and after a charged moment of silence the bustle recommenced in a more subdued fashion. The women turned to the display of vegetables and the men studied the choice of cigarettes and tobacco with great interest.

Lucy's greeting was returned politely but most of the women avoided her eyes awkwardly, and nobody stepped forward to speak to her until Mrs Hamble leaned across her wooden counter at the far end of the shop. 'My dears, how terrible for you,' she said sympathetically in her soft voice. 'That poor man.'

Reflecting yet again on how quickly news travelled round a small village, Lucy answered her quietly, 'Yes, indeed, Mrs Hamble. We can't imagine what we're going to do without him.' The villagers' reticence disappeared immediately and they crowded up to the counter, anxious not to miss anything and eager to ask questions.

'Such a pleasant man. Do they have any idea who did it, Lucy?'

Lucy had no chance to reply before somebody else chipped in, 'It'll be one of those wandering tramps, you mark my words.'

'Umm, not seen any of that like about here for a whiles, I haven't,' another voice said doubtfully.

Mrs Hamble ignored the general turmoil and spoke again, raising her voice to carry above the hubbub. 'He'll be buried here, I suppose?'

Lucy nodded. 'Yes, in the priory cemetery, if we can get permission. He would have liked that.'

Mrs Hamble agreed, 'Aye, that he would, and there'll be a fine turnout for him too. Apart from the ghouls,' she added disparagingly, 'for he was a good man, although not perhaps always an easy one.'

That, thought Lucy, would appear to be Graham's epitaph. And, after all, not a bad one. She said evenly, 'Yes, he was. Meanwhile, we're a bit at sixes and sevens but we still need to eat. Can I have five pounds of potatoes, please, some carrots,' she paused, peering through the crowd to the vegetable crates, 'some of the sprouts and, umm, some of the early strawberries.'

Mrs Hamble's young son unceremoniously elbowed his way through the throng, pushing Lucy's basket in front of him without compunction, and began to collect the vegetables. Will stayed stubbornly at Lucy's side, jostled and pushed from time to time, but as she continued her shopping his attention wandered. He watched the avid faces of the other shoppers with curiosity and realised that they were all lingering in the shop far longer than they usually did. He did not miss the glances that were shot slyly at himself and Lucy from time to time, and occasionally he caught a hissing whisper. His cheeks began to grow warm and he was glad when Lucy had finished at last and he was able to carry the laden basket out of the door.

He waited until they were out of earshot and then burst out angrily, 'It's horrid. Did you see how they were all watching us?'

'Will, it's only natural.' Lucy tried to pacify him. 'However horrid it is, and they do find it horrid too, it's still a big excitement for them. They're not involved in it, you see, but we are, so we're a great source of interest to them. I expect it'll wear off soon,' she finished optimistically.

'Do you mean they really think we did it?' Will demanded.

'Me, Will, not us,' Lucy corrected him gently, 'and no, I shouldn't think so, not really, but after all we've been speculating about who could have done it. It's just the same for them.'

Will opened his mouth to refute this with some passion, but was foiled as Anna drew up beside them in her father's battered Landrover.

'Darlings, I'm just coming over to see you with commiserations, mine and Daddy's.' She leaned out of the window. 'I know he was a bit of a pain, but not a nice way to go.' She glanced at them, and continued lightly, 'I've had a very civil inspector with a rubicund sidekick up at the house, asking me all sorts of questions about my movements on the crucial night. I was definitely left with the impression that he thought I'd done it. Do you think he has that effect on everyone?'

Lucy could not help smiling at Anna's expression of comic dismay. 'Probably. I should think we all feel a little guilty when confronted by the police, whatever it's about.'

Simon spoke from behind them. 'Lucy, I swear I thought they were going to put the cuffs on by the time they'd finished with me. That red-faced sergeant's fingers were twitching uncontrollably.'

Will put the heavy basket down with a thud and resigned himself to a long wait, but Anna gurgled with laughter. 'Simon, not you too. What have you been doing?'

'It's what I didn't do,' he explained. 'I didn't invite an audience to watch me fire my pots last night. Ergo, I could have been out thumping Graham on the head.' Will muttered something under his breath, but Simon carried on, 'I can't help nourishing a slight wish that Graham had been wandering around at a more reasonable time.'

'As things have turned out, we must all wish that,' Lucy said dryly.

Anna intervened quickly. 'Well, Daddy has let me down. He'd gone to bed by the time I got in, and I especially went home early to sit with him too. As the old dear can't swear to when I got back I haven't got an alibi either, and I'm sure the police are nurturing a suspicion that I could have slipped out, or just not gone in at all when I was dropped off.' She smiled sunnily at Simon, 'They'll probably make us accomplices soon.' She saw that Lucy was looking strained and was instantly apologetic. 'But it must be far worse for you, my pets. Is there anything I can do? I'm also bearing offers of help from Daddy.'

'Thank you, Anna,' Lucy replied gratefully. 'It's very kind of you both, but there's nothing really. Hugh is advising us, which is a help, but the police are being very good.'

'Ah yes, of course, Hugh is rather special in that line, isn't he?' Anna said.

Simon looked puzzled. 'You've lost me. Why is Hugh involved? Is he a suspect too?'

'Stupid.' Anna retorted. 'He's famous,' she exaggerated blithely, 'a famous lawyer renowned for his cases. He was involved in that one all over the papers a couple of years ago. What was it,' she mused, then brightened, 'I know, the Benton Case.'

'He's a barrister,' Will corrected her.

'I see,' Simon said, taken aback. 'Well, maybe we'd all better come round for a spot of advice.'

Anna sighed. 'It's an ill wind, too. Daddy feels so guilty about not being able to give me an alibi that he's agreed to stump up the money for a trip to Paris. But now I can't go.'

'Why not?' Lucy asked.

'Well, that wretched policeman said I could move about locally, but asked me, or really told me, not to go out of the district. I rather think he'd class Paris as a bit far,' she said pensively.

'Hard luck, Anna,' Simon commiserated. 'I got a similar warning too, but I'm taking some work in to the gallery in

Coombhaven tomorrow. After all, I've still got my living to earn. Look,' he added impulsively, 'why don't you come for the ride? I'm sure that'll be classed as local.'

'That's a good thought,' Anna said. 'I'd like to come.' She turned to Lucy. 'Would you like me to run you up to the house with the shopping? Will looks heavily laden.'

'Thanks, Anna, but we're quite glad of the walk,' Lucy replied, to Will's relief. 'We'd better be getting back though, or Gran will be wondering where we've got to.'

Anna nodded. 'Fine, but remember where we are if you need us.'

Simon chipped in, 'That goes for me too. You know I'll do anything I can.' Lucy was just about to speak when he added, 'Here comes Tilly, nose twitching.'

Anna glanced along the street. 'Get off, Lucy. We'll try to distract her.'

With brief farewells, Lucy and Will turned gratefully in at the manor gateway. 'I wouldn't be surprised if somebody murdered Tilly,' Will said savagely. 'And Anna too. I bet that's why her father's paying for her to go away. He's afraid she'll be next.'

In spite of herself, Lucy laughed. 'She's alright, Will. She's a good friend.'

Will grunted in disbelief, but his face brightened almost immediately. 'Look, there are Hugh and Mike!' He waved his arm vigorously as the two men came down the footpath from the priory gatehouse.

'Hello, Lucy,' Hugh said as they approached, giving Will a friendly glance as he saw the heavy basket the boy was clutching. 'We're just coming up to see how things are going.'

Mike nodded his head of tousled red hair. 'Yes, surely the police must have got a bit further by now. What an appalling thing to happen.'

They started to walk slowly along the drive towards the house, but were startled by the crunching of gravel under hurrying feet behind them. 'Lucy, Lucy!' Tilly's high voice sounded breathless as she hurried up to them.

With a resigned glance at Hugh, Lucy turned to greet her. 'Hello, Tilly.'

'How glad I am to catch you,' Tilly panted, her bloodshot eyes surveying Mike with unfeigned interest. 'I do hope I'm not interrupting anything. I was just coming up to see what was happening, at least,' she amended hastily, 'to see if there is anything I can do.' Mike's blue eyes narrowed as his gaze raked her from head to foot, and she suddenly seemed disconcerted.

'That's very kind of you, Tilly,' Lucy said carefully, 'but there's nothing anyone can do at the moment, thank you.'

'Oh, I'm sure there must be all sorts of little things,' Tilly said brightly, recovering her equilibrium. 'I was going to call in on Jack,' she glanced back at the lodge, where there was no sign of anyone, 'but I'll come on up with you instead and have a word with your grandmother.'

'Not now.' Mike spoke abruptly. 'Lucy is too polite to tell you to go away, but we've business to discuss and you'd be in the way.'

'Well!' Tilly gasped. 'Well, really!' She stood gaping, for once completely lost for words.

'Come on, Lucy, don't stand here dithering,' Mike said, taking her arm and pulling her unresistingly along the drive. After a startled look at Hugh, Will hurried after them, trying to contain the laughter that was bubbling up inside him.

'We're all finding it stressful, Tilly,' Hugh reassured her. 'Why don't you come up some other time?'

Before she had time to catch her breath he strode off, quickly overtaking Will. One glance at Hugh was enough, and the boy broke into loud laughter. Mike stopped, his hand still on Lucy's arm so she, perforce, had to stop as well. He turned round to stare at Will and then he too broke into a roar of laughter.

Hugh's eyes met Lucy's. 'You must admit that Mike's methods are effective,' he said.

She gazed at him for a second and then her gamine smile lit her face. 'Yes, but poor Tilly.'

'Nonsense,' Mike said robustly, ceasing to laugh. 'There's never any point in handling people like her with kid gloves.'

Hugh looked at his friend mockingly. 'Do you handle anybody with kid gloves?'

Mike snorted. 'Shouldn't need to, people should be able to stand the truth. If they're fools, they must expect to be told so.'

Will agreed heartily. 'She's the one who's got some batty ideas about ghost-hunting in the priory, you know.'

'What!' Mike's exclamation was explosive. 'What's this?' Will began to explain and they moved on down the drive at a brisk pace.

'Is he always like that?' Lucy asked.

'Yes, at least ever since I've known him,' Hugh replied, 'and that's several years.' Silence fell for a while, then Hugh said, 'I didn't know Will was so keen on shopping.'

Lucy smiled. 'You know he's not. He didn't feel I should go down to the village on my own.'

'And he was quite right,' Hugh replied firmly. 'It won't be pleasant for a bit, and his support will be very useful.'

Lucy set her lips tightly and he thought at first she was not going to reply, but suddenly she capitulated. 'Yes, it was good to have it this time. I know the interest will wear off, especially when the police catch the man who did it, but it was rather awful.'

'It'll probably get better each time,' Hugh reassured her, 'but let me know if Will can't go and I'll come with you.'

She glanced at him, startled. 'Oh, that won't be necessary, Hugh. I can manage.'

He held her eyes for a moment before replying, 'I know you can. But you don't always have to manage alone.' Her eyes fell as the colour rose in her cheeks, and she bent her head a little so that the heavy curve of hair fell forward, hiding her face. Hugh put his hand on her arm, drawing her to a halt, and turned to face her. 'Lucy.' When she did not look up he put his other hand under her chin, forcing her head up until her eyes met his. 'Promise me, Lucy.'

She stared at him. 'Alright,' she said in a low voice. 'I promise.'

For a second longer he held her, then as he bent towards her they were both startled by Will calling them from the courtyard. 'Come on, you two! Gran's got tea waiting.' Hugh released her without comment and they walked on in silence to the house.

Isobel Rossington was seated at the desk in the sitting room when they entered. Mike was sprawled comfortably in one of the armchairs, regaling her with the story of his interview with the police. Juno lay at her mistress's feet but came daintily over to greet Lucy, while Hades tore himself away from Mike's side and rushed over to welcome them, his long tail waving furiously. Lucy stooped to pick up Juno, hugging her closely with bent head as she sat down, and Hugh crouched down beside Hades for a few minutes, pulling the big dog's ears gently, before seating himself.

Undeterred by their arrival Mike continued his tale, pausing briefly from time to time to drink his tea. Lucy noted with amusement that he had a large mug, knowing that her grandmother usually disapproved of them in the sitting room. 'It was rather a shock to find the police waiting for me at Hugh's,' he was saying. 'My first thought was about that wretched road tax, I still can't remember whether I've renewed it or not,' he added in an aside to Hugh. Turning back to Isobel he said, 'I gather that I saw the same blokes as you all did. Do you think they're competent?'

Without waiting for an answer, he suddenly turned to Hugh again. 'They seem to think Graham's death has something to do with our discussions about the priory. I'm blowed if I can see why.' He frowned. 'I hope they're not going to damned well interfere.' Hades sat down in front of him and put a large paw on his knee. Mike grinned at him. 'No, it's alright, old chap, we'll have lots of diggings for you to sniff round.' Hades wagged his tail appreciatively and they all laughed.

'There are other possibilities too,' Hugh said, 'and possibly more dangerous ones.' Will turned quickly to look at him from his stance on the hearthrug, and the women looked startled.

'So tell us then, Hugh, what you got out of the police,' Mike said, staring at him.

'It definitely isn't to go any further,' he warned them and, seeing them all nod soberly, he briefly repeated the account Inspector Elliot had given him.

'I can't believe it,' Lucy said when he had finished. 'Surely we'd know if the priory was being used?'

'Not necessarily,' Hugh replied, 'not if people were only resting there overnight.'

'Why ever didn't Graham mention his suspicions to us?' Isobel lamented.

'Because he wasn't sure himself, he'd only his gut instinct really, and,' Hugh said gently, 'he didn't want to worry you.'

'Do you think it's Tilly?' Will sounded hopeful. 'And Anna's come back quite unexpectedly,' he added, scowling as Lucy laughed.

Addressing Hugh again, Mike said, 'Well, there's only one thing for it. If the police can't get it sorted out we'll have to see to it. I can't have our plans upset.'

'I don't think it'll come to that. Fortunately,' Hugh said sardonically, 'Elliot knows his stuff and it would be better not to get in his way.'

Will began to enthusiastically endorse Mike's idea but his grandmother intervened, picking up the paper that she had been working on. 'I've just written this obituary notice for the papers. Would you all like to look through it and see what you think.'

They gathered round her, reading through the short paragraphs and nodding in approval. 'In that case,' Isobel Rossington said, 'I'll send it off.'

'Shouldn't we show it to Jack?' Lucy asked.

'Probably,' Isobel said. 'But I don't know where he is; there was no reply when I rang the lodge. I don't expect he'll be at all agreeable about it anyway.' She turned to Hugh. 'Now, what about some tea? You'd probably like some more too,' she said to Mike.

They both accepted immediately, and Will said happily to his sister, 'Let's have some cake. It's chocolate, your favourite.'

'I'm not surprised,' Mike commented, licking his finger to pick up the crumbs on the plate he had balanced on his lap, before passing it to Lucy for another slice.

Will tossed restlessly in his bed. His mind flitted backwards and forwards from Graham's death to the various plans Mike had suggested during the evening. He turned over again but could not seem to get comfortable, whatever position he lay in. At last he lay as still as he could, hoping that he would fall asleep, but a thin beam of moonlight peeped through a chink in the curtains and shone tantalisingly on his face. Heaving a great sigh he got up, avoiding Hades as he lay on the rug beside the bed, and went to the window overlooking the front drive. Pausing for a moment, he drew the curtains back, grateful for the cool breeze blowing through the open window onto his heated body.

The moon was almost full and lit the landscape with an eerie clarity. As he gazed at the strangely unfamiliar sight a long drawn wail sounded from beyond the brook, and Will was instantly wide awake, suddenly reminded of the owl.

Hastily he dragged off his pyjamas and scrambled into jeans and a sweatshirt. Hades sat up, his bright eyes gleaming alertly. Will thought for a minute and then decided. 'No, Hades, stay, there's a good boy.' The black dog stared at his master in disbelief. 'Stay, Hades,' Will repeated softly. The dog lay down with a heavy thump and Will muttered again, 'Good boy.'

He opened his door cautiously, knowing that the hinges would squeak noisily if he pulled it too far back, and crept down the east stairs, avoiding the treads that creaked, to the corridor by the study. He carefully drew back the bolts on the side door and unlocked it, taking the key with him as he opened the door. Moonlight shone down outside, making it almost as bright as day. Moving quietly, Will shut the door and locked it, pocketing the key before running down the lawn to the track that joined the main drive.

Once there he trod more freely, less worried about disturbing his family, and he soon reached the prior's bridge. A momentary qualm shook him and he paused indecisively. Nonsense, idiot, he castigated himself fiercely, the murderer won't dare to come back so soon. At last he gritted his teeth, crossed the bridge and pushed his way through the bushes, studiously avoiding the path where he had found Graham.

At the north-western corner of the old priory he slowed down, breathing rather heavily, and tried to move more quietly. After all this trouble he did not want to frighten the bird away. Keeping to the bushes, he worked his way carefully around beside the lake and at last ended up facing the granary. Choosing a sheltered spot in the shrubbery, he sat down with his back resting against a tree and waited patiently.

He was rewarded in a very short time as a ghostly white shape flew silently across the clearing below the granary and up to perch in the small arched opening near the top of the wall. Will heard an instant cacophony of shrieks and asthmatic wheezings, and hugged himself in delight, realising there were babies in the nest. Thinking of how interested Hugh would be, he watched as the adult bird disappeared through the opening, reappearing shortly afterwards and flying away again on silent wings towards the farmyard.

Will occasionally heard her haunting hunting cry sound again through the night air. She returned regularly, always greeted by the same demanding chorus, and sometimes as she paused, framed in the opening, he could make out the dangling tail of a small corpse gripped fiercely in her beak.

It was quite a while later that Will sat up with a sudden start, realising in alarm that he had fallen asleep. He glanced automatically at his wrist, but found to his annoyance that he had left his watch behind. He got stiffly to his feet and looked around. It did not seem much lighter, so maybe he had not slept for very long. He decided, though, that he had better get back quickly before anyone woke up, because there would be an almighty fuss if they found he had been out in the night.

He was less cautious about making a noise as he followed the path back through the bushes, but the thick leaf mould on the ground made his progress fairly silent. He reached the spot where he had found Graham laying beside the path before he realised where he was, and inadvertently his steps slowed and stopped. Only briefly, but long enough to hear the clear sound of metal on stone ring through the still night.

Will froze with excitement and his eyes widened, as he thought with a sudden stab of fear that the intruder had after all come back to try again. Carefully he edged his way through the bushes until he reached the main track. He hesitated, knowing that he should go and wake the others. But, he argued silently with himself, then the intruder might get away. Having quietened his conscience, he assured himself that he would just creep up and get a look at him, and maybe see what he was doing.

Cautiously, keeping to the cover of the bushes and treading carefully on the grass, he edged towards the prior's gateway. Here the going was more difficult as the gravel track stretched right up to the walls on each side, but Will was as careful as he could be and was certain he had made no noise. He reached the shadow of the arch and paused, his heart thumping so loudly that he could not hear anything else.

Slowly, afire with anticipation and a delicious touch of fear, he peered round the arch, poised to turn and run if he was spotted. He had a clear view along the west cloister and his disappointment was immense when he saw that there was nobody there.

Will's heart sank as he realised the intruder must be in the north cloister, which would be far more difficult to creep up to unobserved. He almost felt like going back to the house, but stiffened his resolve fiercely by thinking of Graham, feeling sure that they would never catch the murderer if he did not find out now who was in the old priory.

Stubbornly he stood in the shadow of the arch and scanned the ground, trying to work out how he could approach the north cloister undetected. At last he decided he would be better off in the garth, where he could dodge between the carts and other farming equipment. Anyway, he thought, it would be better out there than being caught in the west cloister if the intruder suddenly came round the corner.

He stepped resolutely out from the sheltering shadow and set off, scanning the far cloister carefully, darting from cover to cover until he was close to the north aisle entrance. No light showed through the weathered arches and Will was puzzled. Although the moonlight was certainly strong enough to see by outside, he would have thought the man would need a torch inside the aisle.

A chilling thought struck him. Perhaps he had been noticed. Will shrugged, thinking impatiently that he couldn't stay there all night so he'd better get on with it.

He slid silently up to the entrance arch and peered around it, quickly looking both ways, only to find this aisle as empty as the west one had been. Puzzled and frustrated, he leaned back against the cold stone. He was absolutely sure he had heard somebody. So where on earth were they, he wondered, gazing around, and then he suddenly stiffened.

In the church a faint light was flickering. Without pausing for thought, Will darted back across the quadrangle to the prior's gateway. The church door was firmly shut, but he leaned against it, carefully lifting the iron ring to ease the heavy wooden door open a sliver. He slipped silently through and pressed his back to the wall.

Moonlight shone through the clear glass windows and illuminated the small nave. There was nobody to be seen, so Will eased himself away from the wall, swallowing hard. He walked carefully up the nave, keeping well into the centre, scanning each line of benches carefully before he passed them. As he neared the east end he shivered as a draught of cold air crept over him.

Uncertain where this came from, he stood still and surveyed the small family chancel to the south of the altar. The intruder could not be anywhere else unless, of course, he had left by the south-west door before Will entered the church. Will hesitated, unsure now of what to do. He took an uncertain step forward and gasped in sudden pain as he stubbed his toe hard.

Looking quickly down, he drew in his breath with a sharp hiss of surprise. The stone slab covering the crypt had been lifted and a black hole gaped in the floor. Eagerly Will looked down into the darkness, trying to peer beyond the first few steps that were the only visible things in the gloom.

A sudden movement in the air above his head warned him, but too late. A heavy blow stunned him and he felt himself falling forwards, putting his hands out in a vain attempt to save himself, but tumbling down and down into black emptiness.

SEVEN

Neither Lucy nor her grandmother slept late that morning. They sat round the kitchen table in companionable silence, crunching toast and sipping from their coffee mugs. 'This won't do,' Isobel said at last. 'Hugh was right, you know. The police will carry on with the search for Graham's killer, and we must start thinking of our own plans.'

'Yes, I know, but I can't see how we're going to manage.' Lucy was unnaturally despondent. 'Graham was a pain about anything new, but he had every detail of the estate business at his fingertips. We could rely on him to run it and bring in some cash, and that would have funded us while we get our projects working.'

She looked at her grandmother bleakly. 'None of us can run the estate as well as Graham, so the whole house of cards will come tumbling down around our ears.'

'Nonsense, dear.' Isobel spoke briskly, and Juno glanced up from the bowl she was licking clean. 'This isn't like you at all. It's true that none of us know very much as yet about running the estate, but we can learn.'

'Yes,' Lucy agreed, 'but it will take time, and we don't have much of that either.'

'But, Lucy, you don't realise, we do have some.' Isobel leaned forward across the table, clasping her mug between her hands.

'Graham's systems for running the estate aren't going to collapse immediately without him. Problems will arise gradually, and we should have time to grapple with them and learn as we go.'

Lucy was silent, thinking about this, and her grandmother went on, 'And in the circumstances, Will may be right about not returning to Gudwal's. If he's here in the evenings, he'll be able to help too. Where is Will?' she demanded. 'Surely he hasn't slept in?'

Lucy glanced up. 'I wouldn't have thought so, but I didn't hear him moving about when I came down.'

'Well, I think he should be here while we're discussing the future,' Isobel said. 'Would you go up and ask him to get a move on, dear.'

Lucy got obediently to her feet. 'He's never short of ideas anyway, and sometimes they're worth listening to.' She was away for about five minutes, and Isobel raised her head from the sheet of notes she was scribbling as she heard Lucy running back down the west stairs. She appeared in the kitchen, slightly flushed, followed by Hades, who looked round the room hopefully.

'What is it?' her grandmother asked sharply. 'Will?'

'I don't know,' Lucy was breathless. 'He's not in his room.'

'Then he probably got up early and went out,' said Isobel, relieved. 'I expect he couldn't sleep. No need to worry, Lucy.'

'I'm not sure,' Lucy said slowly. 'Why didn't he take Hades? And ...' she stopped.

'Well?' Isobel demanded.

'I think he may have gone out quite early. His bed isn't even warm and his pyjamas are in a heap by the window. He hasn't used his face cloth or his toothbrush, they're only a little damp.'

'Lucy, what's so unusual about that?' her grandmother said. 'I'm afraid you're letting this business prey on your mind.'

Lucy spoke quickly. 'When did you ever know Will to miss a meal? And it's nearly nine now.'

Isobel's brows drew together. 'Yes, that's true, but then Will is very prone to forget the time if he gets involved in something interesting.'

'I'm going to see Hugh,' Lucy said abruptly, and her grandmother looked at her in surprise.

'Alright, dear, if it makes you feel happier, but I'm sure Will is going to turn up as soon as he's hungry.' She glanced at Hades, who was scratching at the door, whining anxiously. 'Let the dogs out as you go, please,'

Lucy picked up a light jacket as she went through the hall, and opened the big oak door, letting the dogs rush out before her. She hurried across the courtyard, round the estate office and onto the track past the east wing that led to the priory buildings. She walked quickly through these as far as the gatehouse without a second thought, then paused and turned back.

She strode along the cloister aisles, looking around anxiously, but finding nothing out of place she went on, almost running in her haste. She thought how silly she was being, but although she had not found anything suspicious in the cloisters she was still just as worried. Well, she told herself defiantly, maybe I'm making a fuss about nothing, but I'm really sure that something's wrong. 'Blow Will!' she said crossly out loud.

She was breathless and pink in the cheeks by the time she walked up the path to Hugh's cottage and banged loudly on the front door. Hugh opened the door almost immediately, and his expression showed instant consternation as soon as he saw her.

'Lucy! What's wrong?' He took her arm. 'Come in and sit down.' He drew her into the sitting room and pushed her into a chair.

'What's up?' Mike spoke from the doorway, where he stood with a steaming mug of tea in his hand. His red hair was wildly tousled, but his blue eyes were bright with curiosity as he looked at Lucy.

'It's Will,' Lucy said, gripping the arms of the chair and leaning forward. 'He's not at home, and I think he may have gone out in the night.'

'Why?' Hugh demanded immediately, and Lucy explained again.

Mike laughed. 'He's sneaked out after something. Clever work,' he said appreciatively, 'but why worry about him yet?'

'You think we should, Lucy,' Hugh said, watching her closely. 'Why?'

'Oh, I don't know.' She held her hands together tightly. 'Gran thinks it's nerves, and maybe it is, but I'm sure there's something wrong. For a start, Will's never missed a meal and I can't see that he'd begin today.'

'Probably took something with him,' Mike suggested. Hugh looked at Lucy, raising an eyebrow in query.

'I don't know.' She shrugged uncertainly. 'He does sometimes, but he knows there's so much to talk over today. And,' she added, 'he left Hades behind. That's unheard of.'

'He's probably back by now,' Mike said, while Hugh regarded Lucy with a frown in his eyes. He walked over to the telephone, picked up the receiver and dialled the manor number.

'Isobel, this is Hugh. Is Will back?' A mumble of words, and then Hugh said, 'I see. We'll be right over.'

Mike had strolled to the fireplace and was leaning against the mantelpiece watching Hugh. He put his mug down as Hugh replaced the receiver. 'Action?' Hugh nodded. 'Righto. Order the troops.'

Lucy's throat felt tight and her voice sounded strange in her own ears. 'He's not there?'

'No,' Hugh replied. 'And your grandmother says that Hades hasn't returned either.'

'You do think there's something wrong then?' Lucy asked in a strained tone.

'I don't think it would hurt to look around,' Hugh replied guardedly.

'Where?' Mike asked. 'Couldn't the boy have gone anywhere?'

'Yes,' Hugh said, 'but he's unlikely to have intended to go far. I think there are two main possibilities. He could have had an accident. He could also have seen something in the priory connected with Graham's death.'

'I see.' Mike's voice was cold. 'Then let's get going.'

'Just a minute.' Hugh looked at Lucy. 'Did you come here first?'

'Yes, of course,' she replied, staring at him in surprise, and he regarded her with a strange expression. 'At least,' she continued, slightly flustered, 'I looked round the cloisters quickly on my way.'

'Then let's see if Simon's in, or Jack.' He turned to his friend. 'Mike, go along the street to the Old Wheelwright's and see if you can get hold of the potter. If you can't make him hear in the cottage, try the studio in the back garden.' He deliberately held his friend's eyes with his own for a moment. 'Have a good look round and if he's not there try to find out where he is.'

'Why?' asked Lucy.

'We may need as much help as we can get,' Hugh said bluntly, and she bit her lip.

'Whether he's there or not, try the lodge on your way back. You may find a rather bolshy chap called Jack there, who may or may not want to help. See what he says.'

'Wouldn't it be easier to ring them?' Lucy asked suddenly.

Hugh looked at her and said, 'Yes, it probably would.'

'Then ...' she fell silent, her face stiffening in shock.

'And where will you be?' Mike asked his friend.

'Up at the manor. We'll go on foot, looking through the bushes in case Will has had an accident. But I think the priory is likely to be the place to search. If we can't find the boy there, we'll need to call in reinforcements.'

'The police?' Lucy asked quietly.

'Yes, I think so. But we'll see what we can find first. Mike, when you come back, bring the car up to the manor in case we need it.' Mike nodded and set off rapidly from the cottage.

Lucy and Hugh followed and glimpsed him striding towards the village as they turned off the track into the bushes around the lake.

Lucy and Hugh reached the manor without seeing any trace of Will. They found Isobel Rossington waiting anxiously for them. 'No sign?' she asked at once, and they shook their heads. 'Lucy, did you go out of the east door this morning?'

'No,' Lucy said. 'Why?'

'The bolts are drawn back and the key is missing. I went to check it after Hugh rang. So that must be the way Will went out.' She turned to Hugh. 'What do we do now?'

'I'm afraid that you must stay here in case he does turn up,' he replied, 'while Lucy and I begin to search the priory. Send Mike along to join us when he arrives, would you?' Isobel nodded and watched them walk away purposefully round the east wing.

'We'll check the barn and the granary first,' Hugh said. 'If we don't find anything there we'll be left with the main priory buildings.'

It took them very little time to look through both these places, and they were returning to the gatehouse when they heard quick footsteps in the entrance quadrangle. Lucy stopped and glanced at Hugh, who said, 'It's probably Mike.' Her face fell, and they moved on.

Mike's red hair suddenly flared against the ancient stonework as he stepped out of the gatehouse to meet them. 'No luck?' he asked.

Hugh shook his head. 'And you?'

'No sign of either of them. The potter went off early according to a neighbour, but she didn't know where he was going. What now?'

Hugh looked around. 'We're left with the priory buildings and the church. Maybe we'd better split up, as we'll all be in hail of each other.'

'Have you checked the chapter house?' Mike demanded suddenly.

'No,' Hugh admitted. 'I'd forgotten about that.'

'He couldn't get in there,' Lucy said. 'It's kept locked.' The two men looked at her in surprise, and she explained, 'The walls are dangerous, you see, so we had to make sure nobody could get into it.'

'Hmm,' Hugh looked thoughtful, 'still, it might be just as well ...'

'Listen!' Lucy interrupted. They all fell silent and the sound of frenzied barking carried clearly to their ears. 'Hades!' Lucy exclaimed. 'He's found Will!'

'This way,' Hugh said, breaking into a run and leading them through the cloister garth. They found the black dog scratching desperately at the closed door of the church. He turned as they approached and whined anxiously, before throwing his body against the stout door.

'Alright, old boy,' Hugh spoke soothingly. 'Stand back now. Lucy, hang on to him.'

Lucy grabbed Hades' collar and dragged him back as Hugh turned the iron ring and opened the door carefully. He peered round it before treading down the shallow step into the church. 'Keep hold of Hades for a bit, Lucy,' Hugh said. 'Mike and I will have a quick look down the nave.'

The two men walked through the church, looking along the line of benches as they went. Lucy followed behind, holding tightly onto Hades who was straining furiously at the constraint. Hugh went over to the family chapel, lifting the heavy curtain that concealed it and looking round the small space. Lucy peered past his shoulder and was about to say something when Mike spoke with a note of urgency in his voice.

'Hugh, come and see this.' They went rapidly to his side as he crouched over a large stone in the floor near the pulpit. 'See, here, and here.' He pointed to marks on the stone. 'This has been lifted recently.' He looked up. 'Do you know what's underneath?'

Lucy answered, 'It's the old crypt. Where the priors were buried.' She suddenly shivered uncontrollably, and Hades pulled free from her restraining hand. He rushed to the stone and began to scratch at it frenziedly, whining loudly.

'Surely he can't be down there?' Lucy's voice was horrified.

Mike looked at Hugh, who said, 'We'll need to lift it. How?'

'Crowbars. One each would do it easily.'

Hugh thought for a moment. 'The farm would be the best place. You'd better go, mention my name, but try not to say too much. Go through the gatehouse, it's quicker.' He pulled the desperate dog back from the stone and tried in vain to soothe him.

Lucy only spoke once as they waited. 'If we called, would he hear us if he's down there?'

Hugh answered briefly, 'No, the stone's too thick.'

At last they heard Mike's hurrying footsteps outside, and Hugh turned to Lucy. 'We'll probably need torches. Are there any at the house?'

She nodded and went out quickly, passing Mike in the aisle and leaving the church door open in her haste. They listened for a minute to the sound of her footsteps running back along the track, and Mike looked at Hugh. 'You think he's down there, don't you?'

'I think there's a good chance,' Hugh replied bleakly. 'Now, Hades,' he forced the reluctant dog to sit. 'Stay.' He took one of the crowbars and began to insert it between the slabs of stone, watched anxiously by the big dog, who whined continuously.

Lucy returned just as they were manhandling the stone onto the flags, exposing a black hole. She stood with the two men at the edge of the blackness, peering down, straining to hear.

'Will?' she called softly, and then louder, 'Will!', but there was no response. Suddenly she felt Hades squeezing past her legs, but before she could grab him the dog was scrabbling and sliding down the stone steps into the darkness, whining eagerly. He disappeared from sight, and they listened anxiously.

The sound of movement ceased abruptly and Hades began to bark excitedly. They looked at each other hopefully, but almost immediately the barking ceased and they heard the dog whimpering.

Hugh's face was set coldly as he reached over to take one of the torches from Lucy's clenched fists, gesturing to Mike to take another. 'We'll go down. You'd better stay here.'

'No.' She spoke with determination. 'There's a torch each, and I'm coming too.'

'Then stay back and mind the steps. They'll be fairly lethal.'

He shone his torch downwards, lightening the gloom a little, but only enough to see the top of the stairway. He went down carefully, followed by Mike and then Lucy, who shivered as the chilly air struck her. Hugh had only descended a short way when he stopped and bent down to touch the step he was standing on. He shone the light onto his fingers when he straightened up and Mike leaned forward to look.

'What is it?' Lucy whispered.

'Blood,' was the bleak response.

They carried on cautiously, the torches lighting up more smears on the steps as they passed. When at last they were close to the bottom Hugh gave an exclamation. He ran heedlessly down the rest of the stairway to the huddled figure that lay at its foot.

Hades was crouched beside Will, pawing at him anxiously, stopping occasionally to lick his face. Mike and Lucy too abandoned all care on the last steps and slithered down them to cluster around Will's body.

Lucy cried out and bent over her brother, but Mike caught her and held her back. 'No, wait, let's see how much he's injured before you touch him.'

Hugh looked up. 'He's still alive, Lucy, but quite badly hurt,

I think. Mike, you'd better take a look at him. You know more than I do.'

Mike handed his torch to Lucy, instructing them to keep the light on Will. Pushing Hades gently away, he felt carefully over the boy. 'Lots of cuts on his face, probably from the steps, though no bones broken as far as I can tell,' he said at last. 'But he's had a nasty knock on the head and he's very cold. I think we'd better risk moving him. The cold could well be the biggest danger now.' His eyes ran over the others, but they were both lightly dressed too. 'We'll find something in the church to cover him, even if it's the altar cloth, but we must try to warm him up.'

'Can we carry him or should we fetch something to lay him on?' Hugh asked.

'We'll carry him, it'll be faster.' As he spoke Mike bent down and carefully eased the unconscious boy into his arms. Hades rushed over again to lick Will's face and hands, but moved out of the way as Mike stood up.

Hugh turned to Lucy. 'Run ahead and warn your grandmother. Get plenty of hot water bottles into his bed. And ring the doctor and the police.' She turned without a word and picked her way rapidly up the steps.

'Can you manage him on your own?' Hugh asked. 'I want to have a quick look around.'

'Sure, he's not heavy.' Mike looked at his friend curiously. 'Do you know what's been going on?'

'I'm not sure,' Hugh said reluctantly. 'There's a missing link, and without it none of my ideas fit together.'

'Well, take care, chum. We don't want you to be number three,' Mike said as he carried Will up the steps, lighted by Hugh's torch, and followed closely by Hades.

The doctor came into the sitting room with Lucy and Isobel, and the waiting men got to their feet. 'He's very bad, but Dr

Bishop says he'll pull through,' Lucy said at once.

'Yes, yes, he's a strong lad, and he's got youth on his side. It was a nasty bang on the head, but he's got a good thick skull,' he chuckled at his own humour, 'so there's only a touch of concussion. Some cuts and bruises too, but as you so rightly said,' he spoke now to Mike, 'the real problem was the cold. Fortunately we can deal with that.' He looked round and saw the inspector. 'Ah, there you are. This chap is getting repetitive. A bit of a nuisance, heh?'

Inspector Elliot refrained from answering. 'Is there any chance that the boy could have seen who hit him?'

'Can't tell you that, you'll have to wait to see what he says when he comes round. Though I can tell you that he was hit with something narrow and rounded, wooden I think, from behind. You can make what you like of that.'

'I see. Any idea of how long he'll be unconscious?'

'No. Possibly a few hours, maybe longer.' He looked at Lucy. 'There's no more I can do here. I'll call in again later on, but you know where to get hold of me if you want me.'

Lucy showed him out and returned to the sitting room. Hugh spoke as she sat down. 'Lucy, can you think back to the day I came to tea here, the first time.'

Too weary to query why he asked, she simply nodded.

'Who else was here?' he asked.

She pondered. 'We were, all of the family, and Graham. Anna came, she was just home. Oh, and Simon, because she'd arranged to meet him here.'

'What for?' Hugh demanded.

'They were going to try some metal detecting, don't you remember?' Lucy was alert now.

'Can you recall the sequence of events after everyone had arrived?'

She frowned with effort. 'Graham left when Simon came, and Will went too. I'm not sure which of them went first. Then Simon and Anna went off, and we went to find Graham for your tour of the priory.'

'Do you know where they were going to work?'

'No, not really, but' she went on slowly 'it was probably down by the lake.'

'Why?' the inspector asked.

'That's where Simon had been working for a few days,' Lucy replied. She glanced at Hugh. 'In fact, they must have gone there because Simon found the fish trap, don't you remember?'

Hugh did not reply, but asked, 'How would they be most likely to get there?'

'Well, probably over the prior's bridge and along the path through the bushes,' she replied, puzzled.

'Beside the priory, then?'

'Yes.'

Hugh turned to the inspector. 'That may well be it. You need to get hold of Anna and see whether she can remember what they did.'

'I'll go over now,' the inspector said, getting to his feet.

'But she won't be there,' Lucy said. 'I've just remembered, Simon is taking her into Coombhaven today.' They all turned and stared at her.

'How do you know that?' Hugh demanded.

'They were talking about it yesterday,' Lucy's cheeks whitened as she began to understand the purport of the questions.

'You'd better put out an alert,' Hugh said curtly to the inspector, 'and bring them in. She could be in some danger; she may be the only person who could prove a definite link.'

'Unless she's in it too,' the inspector said judicially, picking up the handset.

'No,' Lucy was definite. 'Not Anna.'

'No, I don't think so,' Hugh agreed.

'Will he hurt her?' Lucy was almost afraid to put the question.

Hugh's face grew bleak as he stared at her. 'Yes, I think he may, if he has time.'

'Then let's get after them,' Mike said urgently.

Hugh glanced at the inspector. 'Yes,' he said, 'I think we should.' He looked at Lucy. 'Do you know where they were going in Coombhaven?'

'Yes,' she replied through stiff lips. 'Simon said he was taking some of his work into the gallery, and offered to take her with him.'

'Ring up the gallery and see if they've been,' Hugh instructed her, and she moved at once to pick up the handset the inspector had just put down. Hugh turned to Isobel. 'Do you have a local map we can look at?' he asked.

'Yes.' She stood up and walked quickly to one of the side tables, rummaged among the piles of magazines and papers, and withdrew a tattered map.

Hugh took it from her with a word of thanks and spread it across the low tea table. He was half listening to Lucy's voice as he beckoned to Mike and the inspector to look at the map with him. They had only been poring over it for a few seconds when Lucy replaced the handset.

They turned as she spoke to them. 'Simon was there about an hour ago, and Anna was with him, helping to fetch in his work. James Grantham, the owner, said they seemed in fine spirits.' She swallowed hard. 'They left half an hour ago.'

Hugh asked sharply, 'Did either of them say what they were going to do next?'

'Not really, but,' Lucy added, 'James thought they both seemed excited. He saw a small rucksack partly tucked under a blanket in the back of Simon's van, and wondered if they were planning a quick trip away.'

Mike uttered a loud expletive, while Hugh stared at her, his brows knitted. Then he turned on his heel and bent over the map once more.

They watched him in tense silence for a few minutes until he spoke to Lucy again. 'Where would you take out a boat if you didn't want to be seen doing it?'

'Well, there are lots of creeks between here and Coombhaven that you could use,' she said reluctantly.

'What about round here?' he demanded.

'Either Rosgully Cove if the tide is high, or our own little quay in the bay.'

Hugh considered. 'The tide is coming in, isn't it, and should be full in about an hour?' Lucy nodded, and he turned to the other two men.

'Right,' he said, 'this is how I see it. Putting together bits and pieces of conversations, I reckon Simon has used the excuse of a boat trip to persuade Anna she can pay a short visit to France.'

'But why?' Lucy demanded.

'She's got the chance to audition for a big role in a new play in Paris, and I think she really believed she'd lose it because she had to stay here until the case is solved.' Hugh was succinct, and glanced across at the inspector as he spoke.

'What?' Elliot ejaculated. 'We wouldn't have kept her away from it. There was never any question of that.'

Hugh sighed. 'I know. I didn't think she was serious when she said it, but I rather fear now that she might have been.' He looked at the inspector ruefully. 'Many people really don't have any idea of police procedure.'

'Alright,' Mike said angrily, 'so she's been stupid. But why do you think the potter's involved in this? He must know she can go over to France any time she wants.'

'Yes.' Hugh said. 'It'll take too long to explain now, but I think he wants to make sure she doesn't go anywhere.'

'Kill her, d'you mean?' Mike demanded harshly.

'I'm afraid so,' Hugh replied flatly, looking again at the map. 'There are too many options for comfort but my gut feeling is he'll try to take her out from here, which narrows the possibilities down to two. And,' he added, 'I think Rosgully Cove could be too public, which leaves the Rossington quay.'

He glanced at the inspector. 'But you should have a search made of all the creeks between here and Coombhaven, as I could easily be wrong. And you should have a watch put on the roads for a green Morris van, in case you can find them before they get to the sea.'

The inspector groaned, thinking of the manpower this was going to require, but Isobel said quickly, 'Couldn't the airbase help? It's surely a case of serious need, and they're always doing helicopter practice over the sea and the cliffs. This could be a useful way of doing some more.'

He looked gratefully at her. 'I'll get in touch with them immediately,' he said, moving towards the telephone again.

'No, don't use that,' Isobel said, and he stopped to stare at her in surprise. 'It may take a while, and we might need the phone too. You can use the one in the office for as long as you need to.'

'A good thought. Thank you.' He strode out of the room, and Isobel turned back to where the others were still conferring.

'Look, Hugh, there's a farm track here leading to Hope Point,' Mike said. 'He could take her down there from the coast road and avoid the village altogether.'

'Yes,' Hugh agreed, 'but he may drop her to walk down, and bring his van back here to avoid any suspicions later that he was involved.'

'Hugh,' said Isobel suddenly, 'shouldn't I ring Anna's father to see if perhaps she's just gone home? After all, we may be getting alarmed without any real reason.'

He glanced at her approvingly. 'Yes. Can you do it now?' She walked quickly across the room and picked up the telephone.

'We should get down to the quay,' Mike said. 'If they left Coombhaven half an hour ago we haven't got any time to lose.'

'If I'm right,' Hugh said grimly.

'Well, we've got no other option than to act as if you are, have we?' Mike demanded. 'Your score is pretty good normally, let's hope your thinking's up to scratch now.'

Isobel put the handset down and turned towards them, looking very serious. 'She isn't at home, and isn't expected back early either. All the colonel knows is that she's gone to Coombhaven.'

'Come on,' Mike said, and strode forward.

Hugh put a hand on Lucy's arm, holding her back. 'No, don't come with us,' he said. 'Go out on the police boat. Make sure they get to Hope Cove as quickly as possible.' She met his eyes for an instant before they turned and followed Mike out of the room. Isobel stood alone, looking after them as she gathered Juno into her arms.

Anna's black curls lifted in the breeze blowing through the open passenger window of the green Morris van. It was bowling down the coast road and she had a wide view of the sea, brilliantly blue under a clear sky. 'It's a glorious day,' she said to the driver. 'I'd almost rather be going sailing.'

'And miss your chance to become famous?' Simon teased.

'Oh well,' she smiled at him, 'maybe not. But,' she added thoughtfully, 'I'm still not sure that the police really meant I couldn't go to Paris. It's not as if it's the end of the earth, after all.'

'It probably is to a police mind,' Simon said lightly. 'You can always ask them if you want, but then we'll have blown this chance if they do say you can't.'

'I suppose so.' Anna sighed, and then brightened. 'Still, it'll be fun to sneak away for a few days.' She looked at him reproachfully. 'I wish you'd let me put together a picnic in Coombhaven. We'll be starving by the time we get to France.'

'The tide, Anna, we don't want to miss it,' he replied.

'No, alright, but really we've got plenty of time,' she said, and then asked, 'What will you tell Lucy?'

'Nothing, if I can avoid it,' he answered. 'I don't mind helping you, but I don't want all and sundry knowing I've done it. The police won't be best pleased if they find out.'

'No, I suppose not,' she agreed, 'but you might drop Lucy

a hint if she's worrying.' She glanced up at the sound of a helicopter. 'Heavens, that's low,' she said. 'The pilots get more and
more daring. I saw one actually land on a very tiny headland
once.'

Simon looked up through the windscreen, craning his head
to get a view of the helicopter, and Anna gave a little scream.
'Look out!' she cried, as the van lurched onto the verge. Simon
pulled it back quickly and Anna relaxed into her seat, looking
across at him reproachfully.

He was rather pale, and biting his lip nervously. 'Sorry,' he
said with an effort, 'I wanted to see what kind it was.'

'Only an ordinary one,' she said, and was startled to hear
him muttering under his breath.

'Was it a naval one?' he demanded abruptly.

'Well, it was khaki coloured,' she replied helpfully. 'Is that
naval or military?'

'Either, I think,' he said, seeming to get over his shock and
speaking more easily. 'Shouldn't the turning be soon?'

'Round the next big bend,' she replied, 'about another couple
of miles. Oh,' she added, 'here it comes again.' The noise grew
louder and louder, and suddenly the helicopter was overhead
again, flying even lower now.

'Bloody hell,' Simon snapped. 'What does the moron think
he's doing?'

'He seems to be following our route,' Anna said calmly.
'Don't let it bother you, Simon, they often do that. I expect it
livens things up a bit if they've got something to make exercises
seem more real.'

He glanced sideways at her, and clearly pulled himself
together. 'Sorry, Anna, they always make me nervous when they
fly too low. Anyway,' he added, 'here we are.' He pulled the van
off the road onto a track that was hidden between two high
blackthorn hedgerows, and turned the engine off.

He got out quickly, glancing upwards, and seemed reassured when he saw the helicopter had gone. He went to the

back of the van and opened a door. Anna strolled round, casually beautiful in black jeans and a chunky dark red jumper, with thick-soled leather ankle boots on her feet. 'Thanks, Simon,' she said pleasantly, putting out her hand for the rucksack. 'I don't think I've ever travelled so lightly before.'

'I'll take it until we get there,' he said, shouldering the pack.

She looked at him in surprise. 'I thought you were taking the van home first.' She smiled at him. 'I do know the way to the quay, honestly.'

He did not smile back, but said, 'I'm worried about the tide. Let's get going.'

She shrugged and did not bother to say that the tide would be fine for the next couple of hours, thinking that Simon really wasn't cut out for adventures if they made him this nervous.

They did not speak, just walked at a steady pace along the track, which went directly towards the cliffs. The helicopter reappeared, crossing and recrossing their path, and Simon swore softly, increasing Anna's growing consternation.

At last the track branched, the main stem going on towards Hope Point and the other down through a shady tunnel of overarching trees to the cove below. Anna, with Simon close on her heels, emerged into the sheltered bay, where the sunlight struck sparks off the white-tipped waves curling over the deep blue water. In front of them was a wide shingle beach, and nearby the remains of an old lime kiln perched beside a small stone quay that jutted out from the cliff into the sea.

The bay was quite deserted, apart from the small boat bobbing quietly at anchor by the quay. Simon glanced upwards into the empty sky before hurrying down towards it, saying sharply, 'Come on, Anna, don't hang around.'

They had nearly reached the boat when a man appeared suddenly, stepping out of the lime kiln ruins onto the quay. 'What the hell kept you?' he demanded of Simon.

'Jack!' Anna said in dismay, her heart lurching. 'What are you doing here?'

He grinned at her unpleasantly. 'I'm coming for the ride,' he said, enjoying her discomfort. 'Such a nice day for a sea trip.'

Anna turned to Simon, who would not meet her gaze. 'You didn't mention Jack was coming,' she said accusingly.

It was the other man who answered nastily. 'He thought you might not want my company.'

Anna looked at him haughtily, her chin raised. 'I don't,' she said, and turned away. 'Give me my rucksack, Simon. I've changed my mind.'

Jack seized her roughly by the arm. 'Too late for that. Get her other arm, Simon,' he commanded, 'and let's get on board.'

The sudden whirring of the helicopter, flying very low above them, distracted Simon for a second. Then he grabbed Anna as well and the two men began to pull her towards the boat.

A shout from the beach brought them to an abrupt halt. They turned quickly, still holding Anna tightly between them. Mike strode forward onto the quay, closely followed by Hugh. 'Okay,' he shouted, 'it's all over. Let her go now.'

'Oh yeah?' Jack yelled unpleasantly, pulling Anna closer to him and moving towards the sea. 'Why should we?'

Hugh caught up with Mike, putting out his hand to draw the other man to a halt just out of range of the trio grouped dangerously close to the edge of the quay.

'Well, well,' Jack sneered, 'if it isn't Mr Barrister, trying to interfere again. Well, this time you'll play my game.' He grinned maliciously. 'I'm calling the cards, so if you want her back safely, you'll stay out of the way.'

Hugh stood relaxed, but ready to move, and replied, 'You haven't a hope, Correll. Why make things more difficult for yourself?'

Mike stood silently beside him, keeping himself well under control and watching the other men with cat-like concentration, ready to pounce at the slightest opportunity. The helicopter flew over again, lower still, and the draught from the rotors made Anna's hair blow out, blinding Simon briefly, so that he relaxed his grip.

Anna jerked herself away from him, but before the others could help Jack swore and grabbed her roughly, yanking her tightly against him. 'Get over here with that pack,' he ordered Simon harshly, 'and get it strapped on to her back.' He glared at Hugh, his eyes bulging with hate. 'Whatever I'm going to get,' he snarled, 'you won't get her. The slightest trouble from either of you and she goes over the edge. Weighted down with that, she won't stand a chance.'

He smiled triumphantly and shifted a little as Simon approached with the rucksack. Anna took her chance and brought her booted foot up heavily behind her, striking unerringly between Jack's legs. As he screamed in pain, releasing his hold on her and doubling up in agony, Anna spun round and jabbed her fingers into Simon's face. He yelled and clutched his eyes, while she ran forward, away from the quay.

Mike and Hugh stood stunned for a second, and then raced to the other men, grasping their arms as they writhed in pain. Then, added to the sound of the helicopter above, came the roar of engines, and three police motor boats powered across the bay towards them. Inspector Elliot jumped ashore from the first boat as soon as it came near the quay, and ran over to them, followed closely by Lucy.

'Well done,' he said, scanning the scene. 'You don't even seem to have damaged them too much.'

Mike stared at him, still a little taken aback, and then he grinned. 'Oh, we barely touched them,' he drawled. 'She did all the damage.' He nodded at Anna, who stood at a distance, the sea breeze blowing the black curls around her blazing white face.

EIGHT

A few hours later Anna sat, pale and composed, in an armchair in the manor sitting room, gratefully sipping at a large brandy.

'It was incredibly stupid,' Mike was saying explosively, 'going off with that man to get yourself quietly murdered.'

Anna looked up indignantly, some of the usual colour returning to her cheeks. 'How was I to know? I don't go round suspecting that people I know are murderers.'

She shivered and Lucy demanded, 'But what happened? I'm still quite in the dark.'

'Well,' Anna was steadily regaining her usual animation, 'it was just like being on a film set, not the sort of thing you think really happens.'

'Get on with it,' Mike snapped, and she scowled at him.

Lucy intervened hastily. 'We know you went to the Coombhaven gallery.'

Anna nodded, looking a little embarrassed. 'Yes, well, Simon had suggested that if I brought a few clothes and my passport with me, we could come back to the quay, collect Bob's boat and slip across the Channel. I'd nip up to Paris for my audition, and he'd pick me up again in a few days. We thought it would be such a short time that the police might not notice.' She shivered again, and took another quick sip of brandy. 'It just seemed a bit of a lark at the time.' She paused, glancing at Lucy, suddenly remembering that she did not know about the play.

'Hugh told us,' Lucy said quietly, and Anna looked at him in surprise.

He nodded. 'Yes, lots of little pieces suddenly all fell together. I didn't realise you really thought the police wouldn't let you go to Paris.'

Anna flushed delicately. 'I didn't truly until I was talking to Simon. I suppose I let him persuade me.' Mike snorted, and she glared at him. 'Alright, it was stupid.'

'Nearly terminally stupid,' he growled, and she sat up straight in her chair.

'I was well able to look after myself,' she said sweetly, and he frowned blackly.

'When did you realise something was wrong?' Lucy asked quickly.

'Well, gradually, I think,' Anna said. 'Simon was oddly jumpy about the helicopter buzzing us, and I suppose I was edgy by the time we got to the quay. Of course,' she added, 'seeing Jack really clinched it.'

She looked across at Lucy and her eyes began to sparkle. 'Wasn't it amazing in the bay! A helicopter buzzing us, three speedboats racing across the water and four men fighting over me.'

Mike's blue eyes narrowed. 'A charming fantasy!' he said sharply. 'You nearly ended up in the sea.' She unwittingly rubbed her arm, and he added crossly, 'You could have had a lot more than a few bruises to worry about.'

Anna had fully recovered her spirits by now. 'Just think, Lucy,' she turned to her friend, 'they think Jack and Simon were going to sling me overboard as we crossed the Channel.'

'But why?' Lucy demanded, bewildered, and they all turned to Hugh.

'They'd thought it out carefully,' he replied. 'Bob's boat was hired in Anna's name, ostensibly for an excursion she discussed in front of me. Once she'd disappeared they hoped it would look as though she'd done a bunk.'

'What!' Anna sat up. 'Why?'

'Oh, for killing Graham and shutting Will into the crypt,' Mike answered nonchalantly.

Anna swung round on him in a sudden rage, and then winced. 'Poor Daddy.'

'Poor foolish little girl,' he snarled.

'But why did they want to get rid of Anna?' Lucy persisted. 'Did they do all the other things too?'

Hugh nodded. 'Yes, it's quite a straightforward story. It all comes down in the end to greed, overwhelming greed, I'm afraid. Simon and Anna found those lead plant tags in the shrubbery by the brook, and they were still there when Graham took me around the priory buildings. We had an interesting conversation, parts of which Simon overheard as there are enough open window spaces for voices to carry quite clearly. In the light of later events, he planned to dispose of Anna because he was afraid she'd overheard it too. She might have been able to link him to it and possibly to all that's been happening.' He grinned affectionately at Anna. 'And of course she can't remember any of it.'

She retorted defensively, 'Well, I just wasn't listening, it all sounded very boring.'

'What did Simon hear?' Mike asked.

'I was puzzled by various aspects of the structure, which suggested to Simon possible hiding places for the prior's treasure. And soon afterwards he found that excavations might be taking place at any time. Hence his need for speed.'

Lucy was aghast. 'Do you mean that he killed Graham because of that hoary old legend? That all this has happened because Simon was stupid enough to believe it?'

Anna's eyes shone as she leaned forwards. 'But of course, Lucy, you came home before us, so you don't know. He found it, and it's at the police station now,' she said, her face glowing. 'Wait until you see it!'

'What ...' Lucy began, but Anna rattled excitedly on, 'Gold, and all over jewels, worth a small fortune, I should think.'

Lucy looked desperately at Hugh, who laughed. 'It's alright, Lucy, she's quite sane.' They heard Mike snort, but Hugh continued, 'The legend was based on fact, you see.'

'Definitely.' Mike said. 'A lovely chalice. It looks like a very skilled piece of work. Fourteenth century French, I should think, although those policemen wouldn't let me have a proper look at it,' he added, aggrieved.

'How did he find it?' Lucy demanded. 'Where was it?'

'His first attempt,' Hugh explained, 'was when Graham was attacked. Simon heard me expressing surprise at the lack of book cupboards in the cloisters, and it occurred to him that they might have been bricked up with the treasure behind, so he tried to find out. An ingenious idea,' he commented dispassionately, as Lucy's eyes widened, 'but wrong.'

He frowned. 'I suspect Graham heard faint sounds while he was walking around and went to investigate. Anyway, Simon didn't hear him approaching until the last minute and only had time to whip out under the arch and grab a stone, wait in the shadows until Graham passed him and then jump out on him.' He sighed. 'Who knows, if he'd had more time to think, perhaps he'd have run off or made up a story. As it was, he just hit him and left him where he fell.'

Hugh's face hardened. 'The attack on Graham was when Jack became involved. That alibi he thought was so clever was instantly suspicious. Elliot certainly traced him to a nightclub in Corrington, but the doorman actually remembers him arriving after two in the morning.' He smiled with satisfaction, adding, 'And he had to stop for petrol. It was clever of Elliot to think of that and find the garage, where Jack is shown very clearly on their security video just before two.'

Hugh glanced at Anna. 'He'd come back from dinner at The Mill in a very bad mood, and found Graham wasn't in. So he went out to look for him, guessing quite correctly that he'd gone to the priory. He bumped into Simon near the gatehouse, just after his attack on Graham. He was probably in a bit of a state, and it wouldn't have taken much for Jack to get the full story out of him. Possibly,' his lips tightened, 'they recognised that they both came from the same mould.'

He turned to Lucy. 'Jack went to see how much damage Simon had done to Graham, and I'm afraid that when he saw it wasn't fatal he decided to help things along. Rather,' he said grimly, 'than raise the alarm, he dragged Graham to where he was found, hoping the delay and the damp would finish off what Simon had started.' He hesitated, and then added reluctantly, 'He may even have used the stone to hit his uncle again.'

Lucy's face was ashen and her hands were tightly twisted together. 'Why?' she asked, her voice unusually harsh.

'Money,' Hugh replied simply. 'Jack was in trouble in London and needed a lot of money badly, which was why he came down in the first place. I think that's why Graham was worrying and wandering around at night, and that's why Jack decided to find him that evening, to press him a bit harder.'

'I can't believe that he'd do that.' Lucy pressed her hands to her face.

Mike looked at Hugh and demanded, 'So which of them is responsible for Graham's death?'

Hugh shrugged. 'That's a nice little problem for the police. I should guess they'll bring a manslaughter charge against Simon, and a murder charge against Jack.'

'At least the bastards won't get away with it,' Mike exploded. 'Trent, the little worm, just went to pieces when he got to the station. He couldn't spit out fast enough that he hadn't meant any of it, it all just happened accidentally, it was all Jack's fault.' He sounded disgusted, and then added with satisfaction, 'But there's no doubt he hit Graham first and left him injured, and probably dying, so he started things off. And none of it would have happened if he hadn't been creeping round the priory in the first place, damaging it as he went.' He ground his teeth loudly as rage boiled up in him at the thought.

Hugh glanced quickly at Lucy and said, 'It was because of Tilly's ramblings that Simon actually tumbled to the truth, you know. The last prior had hidden the chalice with the body of the monk who died just before the Dissolution. He meant to come back himself and retrieve it of course, but, as we know, he was murdered on the cliff path, presumably when he was on his way here.'

He added quietly, 'Will's going to be pleased to have found bones before the excavations even begin.' The others stared at him in astonishment, and he smiled. 'When Mike brought Will back to the house, I stayed behind and had a quick look round.' Mike groaned, and Hugh said reassuringly, 'I didn't touch anything, but the coffin lid was already open.'

Anna gave a little scream, and then said breathlessly, 'Hugh, tell us quickly.'

'There was a wooden coffin on the floor of the crypt, quite close to Will.' Lucy shuddered, but did not say anything so Hugh carried on, 'Simon or Jack had prised off the lid and exposed what I guess are the bones of the last monk.' He glanced at Mike, whose jaws were clenched. 'They don't seem to have been disturbed, the scraps of clothing are still around them, so I guess the chalice was just tucked in beside him.'

The women gazed at Hugh in amazement, and he continued his fantastic story. 'I suspect the tale of the monks walking on the anniversary of their expulsion from the priory is connected with this. The whole of the community here was pretty dissolute from all accounts, and they probably knew, or had a good idea, what the prior was up to. It's quite possible they ambushed and murdered him, but failed to extract the secret of the hiding place from him, so they had to come here whenever they could to search for it. The sight and sound of cowled monks in their old haunts would have been more than enough to keep superstitious locals away.'

'Won't Will love this,' Lucy murmured, and Anna turned

quickly to her. 'How is he, Lucy?'

'He's going to be fine. He's got some colour back already and he's breathing more easily. Dr Bishop isn't so worried about the effects of the cold now.' Her gamine smile suddenly lit up her face. 'And he's well watched over. Gran's sitting with him and Hades is lying at his feet with his eyes fixed on Will's face, positively willing him to wake up. Even Juno is keeping an eye on him from Gran's lap.'

Anna was relieved. 'I'm so glad he's going to be alright. It must have been pretty awful for him, shut up down there, and with an open coffin too.' She shuddered.

'He wouldn't have known anything about it,' Mike said prosaically. 'He was unconscious when he hit the floor. That's probably why he didn't break any bones.'

Lucy spoke suddenly. 'Which of them hit him, do you know?'

'They were almost certainly both there,' Hugh said. 'I can't see Jack trusting Simon to look on his own, and' he added thoughtfully, 'Jack had trade contacts which might have been useful to Simon, which probably made the partnership more acceptable to him.'

The others looked at him enquiringly. 'Elliot made the connection,' he said. 'Jack's father was an antiques dealer who was involved in a case we both worked on a few years ago. He spent a short time in prison, but must be out again now.'

'But,' Lucy persisted, 'which of them hit Will?'

Hugh's lips twisted. 'It could have been either of them, Lucy, and I should think each will blame the other.'

Anna frowned. 'Does that mean they'll get off?'

'Possibly,' Hugh shrugged. 'I don't really know what sort of case can be made against them. There may be sufficient evidence to prove which of them it was.'

'But we can get them for attempting to murder me,' she said with satisfaction. 'There's no doubt about that.'

'Well,' Hugh responded reluctantly, and they all looked at him in astonishment, 'there's no doubt that they were trying to kidnap you, but,' his voice was regretful, 'there's no proof they were planning to kill you, only that they threatened to do so when they were cornered.'

'What!' Mike exploded furiously, cutting off Anna's indignant spluttering. 'What else were they up to then?'

'They could have been smitten with her charms, or planning to sell her into slavery, or hold her to ransom. Oh,' Hugh said abruptly, turning to Anna, 'they could say anything. We'd only have evidence that it really was their intention to dispose of you, if we'd caught them pushing you overboard loaded with weights.'

'And given your fighting skills, they'd have had trouble doing it anyway,' Mike muttered. 'But thank God you got them both where it hurt,' he added with satisfaction.

'Yes, Anna,' Lucy said, 'how did you dare?'

Her friend shrugged modestly. 'Well, d'you remember I did that self-defence course ages ago, when I went to London, because Daddy was so worried about me. Well, it all seemed a bit silly at the time, but when it came down to it on the quay it all just seemed to come back to me.'

Mike was staring at her, his mouth a little open, when a tap at the door startled them. It opened slightly and the inspector peered round it. 'I hope you don't mind,' he said, looking at Lucy. 'I didn't want to knock and disturb the boy. How is he?'

'Oh, doing very well,' she replied. 'Do come in and sit down. We're dying to know what's happening.'

He sat down near the table, where he could look round at them all. He spoke first to Hugh. 'You were quite right about this affair, you know.' He smiled. 'Of course.' Then he added, 'And we've cleared up one strand of that other business I was telling you about.' He looked questioningly at Hugh.

'Lucy and Mike know, but,' he hesitated, 'I think Anna doesn't.' Quickly he outlined the theory about the immigration scam, and then turned back to Inspector Elliot, one brow raised enquiringly.

'There was a strand here, and Trent was the contact,' the inspector said bluntly. 'A boat from further down the coast met the ship on prearranged nights, and brought a few illegals back to the cave you found. They made their way up the tunnel to the top of the cliff, and then along that very hidden track.' His audience were listening, fascinated, and his face was warm with amusement as he went on, 'They split up near the village and each went to different places for their next instructions, and probably clothes and food. The priory buildings were one of these stops. And we've found another.' He paused, savouring his next words. 'That painter woman in the village …'

Lucy and Anna both gasped in surprise, and Lucy said, 'Tilly? Do you mean Tilly Barlow?'

'Yes, that's right,' he said. 'I don't think we'll be able to prove how much she really knew, though. She says Trent spun her some tale about friends of his on walking holidays, but she certainly handed over various packages that he'd given her for them.'

The room was completely silent when the inspector finished, until suddenly Lucy began to laugh, peal after peal of silvery sound. Hugh started up in concern, then, catching her eye, he began to grin, just as Anna's laughter blended with Lucy's. Mike stared at them in surprise, then turned to the inspector. 'Barking,' he said.

Elliot considered him for a minute. 'Have you met Tilly Barlow yet?' he asked quietly.

Mike stared at him. 'I shouldn't think so. Oh,' a thought struck him, 'you don't mean that damned woman who wants to organise ghost hunts in the priory?'

The inspector just nodded, and Mike looked at the others with understanding. 'I see,' he said simply.

At last they stopped laughing, and Lucy wiped her eyes with a tissue, before pushing the box over to the others. 'Won't Will love this?' she asked weakly.

Hugh's mouth twitched. 'A real aid to recovery,' he agreed.

Mike turned to the inspector. 'Have you got the chalice safe?' he demanded.

'Of course,' Inspector Elliot replied patiently. 'I must get back to the station, but we'll need to discuss what to do about it with you and the family.' He addressed Lucy now. 'It's a prime piece of evidence, but you may want to make arrangements about its care, given its antiquity. I'm told,' he glanced at Mike, 'that it needs to be in proper conditions, but I'm sure Professor Shannon will explain that to you.' His voice was level and his face sober, but his eyes twinkled at Lucy, and then he stood up, made his farewells and quietly left the room.

'I suppose I'll have to appear in court,' Anna said meditatively. 'Daddy will just love that.' She put down her glass and stood up. 'I'd better get back to him before he hears about this from anyone else. It's enough to drive him into a frenzy.'

Hugh looked across at Mike, who was propped against the mantelpiece, glowering at Anna. 'Would you run Anna home? I've got some things to tie up with Lucy.'

Mike straightened himself with a bad grace, muttering under his breath, and took Anna brusquely by the arm, leading her out of the room with only time for brief farewells to the others. Lucy had gone to stand by the window and was gazing out thoughtfully. Hugh went over and put his hands on her shoulders, turning her round to face him. 'Do you mind very much?' he asked quietly.

She was surprised into raising her eyes to meet his. She looked puzzled for a second, and then said, 'About Simon? Of course I mind. I liked him, and it's awful to think that he's responsible for all this.'

Hugh studied her face carefully for a moment. 'I was afraid that you liked him too much,' he said deliberately, and she flushed, but kept her gaze steady.

'No, I didn't,' she said, 'but it seemed such an uncomplicated friendship.'

Hugh smiled and his grip tightened, drawing her closer.

'And you wanted to stand four-square on your own independence. Can you bear to let me in?'

She was so close now that she could see the dancing lights in his brown eyes. 'I couldn't bear to keep you out,' she said frankly. He laughed softly and bent his head to kiss her.

They were not sure how much later it was when they became aware of Juno's feathery tail beating lightly against their legs. They drew apart to look down at the little dog, and had just separated when Isobel came into the room.

She glanced at them, eyes widening in surprise as she took in their flushed faces and bright eyes. A slight satisfied smile touched her lips, but she only said, 'Will's awake and completely himself. We heard the cars drive away and we're longing to know what's happened. It's all I can do to keep him in bed, so will you come up now and tell us?'

'Of course,' Hugh said at once, and they both followed her up to the east room, where they found Will propped up in bed, head bandaged, but eyes bright and eager in his bruised face.

'Was it Simon?' he demanded.

'Yes,' Lucy replied simply, carrying on quickly as he showed signs of interrupting, 'and Jack, and Tilly.'

'What?' he said, stunned. 'Are you joking?' he asked, searching her face intently. 'You're not?' He was incredulous as she shook her head.

'Let Lucy tell us, Will,' his grandmother said firmly.

Lucy gave a full account of the affair and then fell silent, while Will sat speechlessly gazing at her. 'Anna did that!' he said at last. 'And Tilly.' His eyes took on a glazed look of immense satisfaction.

Isobel watched them both quietly for some time before speaking. 'Do you realise what this may mean?'

They looked at her, puzzled, and she said, 'The chalice that Simon found. If it proves to be our property it will be worth a lot of money. If we can sell it, it will solve our financial worries, at least for a while.'

Lucy's eyes began to shine. 'Yes, I suppose so.' She smiled. 'Wouldn't Graham be pleased?'

also by MARY TANT

Death at the Priory

Lucy Rossington doesn't need any more trouble just now. She's got plenty of that already at the family manor in an idyllic West Country valley.

So it's really the last straw for her when odd incidents plague the priory excavations, under the controversial leadership of the mercurial Mike Shannon. Does the death of an archaeologist mean more than a temporary disturbance? Is Lucy imagining evil where none exists? She is soon to know.

2008   ISBN 978-1-903152-17-1

Coming soon – the third in the Rossington series

Friends...and a Foe

Life looks promising for Lucy Rossington and her family. There is no way they could guess that in just a few days their happiness might be shattered for ever.

Old friends rejoin the family circle – one of them brings in their wake a secret that somebody would kill to keep. How could the Rossingtons know that this secret will cost them dearly?

Spring 2009   ISBN 978-1-903152-22-5